The Sublime Luminary of Um

Erik Meyer

This book was published and printed in Eau Claire, Wisconsin. Erik Meyer wrote every word, edited the text, and drew the cover art for this book.

First Edition

ISBN: 979-8-9869765-2-5

Dedicated to the 2024/2025 third grade classes of Robbins Elementary and Sherman Elementary.

This is a work of fiction, and the characters, places, and events herein are entirely imagined. Any resemblance to people, locations, or happenings in the real world is entirely coincidental.

This book draws on a rich tradition of literary portal fantasy that has inspired generations of writers to dream of worlds beyond their own.

Current art by the author is on Instagram:

@wiscospeedro

Direct any questions for the author to:

erik.meyer.contracting@gmail.com

The Whiteout

Theodore had come to stay with his grandmother for the holidays, dropped off with presents at the A-frame house on the bluffs that overlooked the Mississippi River. His parents, employed by a startup seed company in central Wisconsin, had scheduled themselves a childless trip to Hawaii, and Theodore did not resent their need for a break, as he had recently turned 10, and, as a single child, could already spot the warning signs of burnout. His mother had bags under her eyes and often forgot to season the stew in the crock pot. His father spent increasing amounts of time in the bathroom and had stopped offering homework help.

Not that Theodore needed homework help.

But he did like being asked.

As a fifth grader, he'd signed up to be a crossing guard at school.

Twice, he'd gotten to read the morning announcements.

For the trip, he'd been told to leave his tablet at home. No electronics. No turning into a zombie; no screen time, they'd said.

So school had let out on a Friday, and his parents picked him up with the car already packed, driving past rows of pine trees until they'd turned down the winding driveway that led to a white-blanketed yard filled with bird feeders. If anything, going to see Grandma Betsy was a welcome change, even if he didn't like the strong smell of the vinegar she cleaned the litter boxes with.

"You know," she said. "You are startlingly handsome."

Theodore spent Christmas Eve and Christmas Day in new sweaters and pajama pants, but by the 26th, after Grandma Betsy finished her crossword, they both needed an outing and went for a drive to town. Since Grandpa Frank had passed, her cat collection had grown. Sadie, a white Persian, was missing her tail. Bobo, a Siamese, chased his shadow.

Between the house and the diner in La Crosse, they had the companionship of Calipso, a piebald longhair who stretched along the windshield, soaking up heat from the defrost.

They stopped for hot chocolate; Theodore looked at books about chess, which he'd played at school but never gotten good at, and by the time they got back on the highway and headed for home, the sun had set with accumulation falling through the high beams.

"Blustery weather," Grandma Betsy said.

Calipso purred and the engine hummed across county road blacktop, Theodore rubbing the cat's belly as his grandmother switched on the wipers.

"Do you think they're hiking up the side of a volcano?" he asked.

"Who?"

"Mom and Dad. In Hawaii."

"Oh. Them."

Rubber blades sped across the windshield, and falling flakes turned to water against warm glass.

Already, snow was drifting into the lane from the shoulder.

"There wasn't anything on the radar," Grandma Betsy said.

"Has Calipso always liked driving?" Theodore asked.

Wind buffeted the car, and the highway vanished, momentarily, replaced by a wall of white.

"Calipso was your grandfather's favorite cat," Grandma Betsy said.

She leaned towards the steering wheel, and as she tapped the brakes, a whiteout engulfed the vehicle.

Blinding white, white like a fresh coat of paint.

Tires left the road, spinning, a smooth exit from pavement, Theodore and Grandma Betsy both frozen in place.

And they waited.

They waited to hit rocks or a guardrail before the vehicle wrapped itself around a tree.

They waited to fly through the front window of a sleepy roadside diner.

They waited for a mailbox to take off the rear-view mirror.

Theodore gripped the shoulder belt and leaned against the door.

Grandma Betsy's knuckles went white.

They waited and waited.

But strangely, the '86 Chevy Celebrity neither flipped on its side nor launched off a bridge.

It sailed through a chalky sea of white, engine idling, supported by a lightness that felt like flying, a smoothness that lasted long enough for both Theodore and his grandmother to become perplexed and wonder what was happening.

"Are we still on the road?" he asked.

"I don't think so," she said.

Engulfed in a blizzard, seconds turned to minutes.

Grandma Betsy found that her cell had no service; the radio played static.

They surged forward, floating in a haze of unchanging light.

"Are we dead?" Theodore asked.

"I don't think so," Grandma Betsy said.

"How would we know?"

"I pinched myself, and it felt like me."

The heater kicked out warmth, and Calipso purred on the dash.

Feeling hot and sweaty, Theodore unzipped his puffy winter jacket.

Confusion, it turns out, can be quite exhausting, and after the initial shock gave way to fatigue, everyone fell asleep, snoozing as the car nosed through colorless space, snoring passengers ferried through a soft glow that carried them to parts unknown.

The Boffins

They awoke to a huge bump followed by bouncing and shuddering, windshield wipers squeaking across spotless glass as the car hurtled down a snowy hill. The vehicle bucked as pine saplings disappeared under the end of the hood, and after clipping a giant stump, smashing through a fence, and crashing through a leaning wooden shed, they limped to the bottom of the incline, grinding to a halt 50 feet from a small community of geodesic dome houses.

"I think we hit something," Grandma Betsy said.

"Just figured that out?" Theodore asked.

"Back a ways," Grandma Betsy said. "At the top of the hill."

And sure enough, through the rear-view mirror, behind the splintered remains of the shed and the fence and the stump, boots stuck up from the white drifts, boots that filled Theodore with a sinking feeling.

"I think you're going to jail," Theodore said.

Almost immediately, people poured from the dome houses, no doubt alerted by the commotion, and Grandma Betsy waved as she opened the car door.

"I have insurance," she said. "It was an accident."

Theodore got out expecting everyone to record them with cell phones and call the police and run to the boots that peeked from the snow and start screaming or at least ask what had happened, but nothing like this happened at all.

Everybody cheered.

Mothers hugged fathers and children and old men with long beards. Elderly women did jazz hands. A bald gentleman raised his arms in the air and then fell back in the powder, kicking up his legs. Gleeful bellows gave way to tears, and as the crowd approached the car, several things became clear:

Firstly, the people from the geodesic dome houses were all very short, and for some reason, they wore matching grayish bodysuits with shiny chrome wrist-bracers. Secondly, they all had blue-tinted skin and over-sized ears and eyes, eyes that shimmered and ears that bounced as they approached the stationary Chevy Celebrity.

Lastly, and this stuck with Theodore in the years to come, everyone was quite skinny, worryingly so, standing with skeletal cheekbones and thin legs, their uniforms hanging off them like clothes on hangers at a box store, everyone huddled together and triumphant like the survivors of an arctic plane crash greeting a rescue convoy.

"What's going on?" Theodore asked.

He turned to Grandma Betsy, who had a confused look on her face and shook her head as a man with white hair and a bushy mustache stepped from the throng. At first, when the man opened his mouth, musical tones escaped, highs and lows with intense vibrato, but after his song went unanswered, he motioned for everyone to quiet down before saying in a high-pitched voice:

"You've done a service to my kin. Our land is stark and cold and dim. My name is Zeb; I give you thanks. What brings you to these snowy banks?"

As Zeb waved his hand in front of the car's headlights, Theodore and Grandma Betsy exchanged glances, her white eyebrows raised above the rims of her glasses, while Theodore's disbelief took the form of an open mouth framed by flushed cheeks while the wind ruffled his short, black hair.

"We've run off the road," Grandma Betsy said. "The blizzard came up so suddenly."

"Where are we?" Theodore asked.

Tapping the car's bumper with his palm, Zeb cocked his head and looked up at the visitors, speaking with giddiness.

"By happenstance," he said. "By fortune's drum,

you've landed in the land of Um. In bondage have we Boffins toiled, maintaining fringe lands long despoiled. Our despot, Governor Eyebright, has made us work both day and night, and with your metal chariot, you've felled a proper idiot."

As Zeb spoke, his people, the Boffins, were already walking up the hill, past the exploded shed and the hole in the fence, past the rotten stump, everyone following the tire tracks to the boots that stuck up from the drifts, and Theodore tagged along, curious in a way he had not been before, as his only previous exposures to crime scenes came from the dramas his parents watched after dinner when he sat on his knees and did his homework on the living room coffee table.

"People aren't usually happy when somebody gets hit by a car," he called to his grandmother.

"Theodore," Grandma Betsy said. "Get away from there."

But even as she spoke, she knew he would see for himself what had been left in their wake, and as the Boffins sang to one another, Theodore nudged the boot heel that poked from a pants leg obscured beneath chunks of compacted snow.

"Found him," he called.

Zeb and Grandma Betsy followed close behind, and as Theodore pushed the boot, it tipped over, spilling ash that caught with the wind and blew away; Boffins picked up the leather duster and the pants and shook out the soot, such that the imprint of the fallen man was quickly reduced to a shadowy impression in a blanket of white.

"Where's the body?" Grandma Betsy said. "What on earth is going on?"

Zeb nodded to the boots, and a Boffin girl picked them up; gray clouds poured out in great plumes, and the girl knocked the heels on her knees before handing them to Theodore.

Zeb turned to them and said:

"'Twas ancient evil kept alive by passions only

negative. The flesh has long since turned to dust. Your fatal blow was fair and just. These footwear relics both are lined with charms beyond the normal kind. Please take the boots, I do entreat. Come join us now. We want to eat."

And with this, Zeb led everyone back to the warmth of the geodesic dome houses and the bubbling pots of soup, for although the Boffins had been forced to live for years on meager rations, they were not about to deprive their new guests of a meal.

Lanterns to Light the Way

Zeb's dome house had throw rugs and cozy cushions for visitors, with heat coming from a potbelly stove in a central kitchen. Mud-caked straw insulated walls broken only by thick glass windows and shelves filled with books written in a script Theodore could not decipher. Everyone ate with wooden bowls and wooden spoons, and after several chats, it became clear that none of the Boffins had ever heard of Wisconsin nor had any ideas about how to get there.

"It's cozy in here, at least," Theodore said.

By now, Grandma Betsy had retrieved Calipso from the car, much to the astonishment and curiosity of the younger Boffins, for they had never seen a cat before, and soon the Boffin children were petting Calipso's furry head, delighted by the soft purring that resulted.

"The crucial thing," Zeb said. "That comes to mind is that you go and find the kind sublime Grand Luminary, for who else can access ancient lore, libraries, knowledge, and archives? Perhaps his grace can change your lives."

"What's a Grand Luminary?" Theodore asked.

Zeb stood and walked to the kitchen, returning with a small, unlit lantern, which he set on an end table. With a press of a button, it hummed and levitated and illuminated, brightness pushing back wall shadows, an even glow washing over dressers and a wardrobe and a pedal-powered sewing machine strewn with fabric and bobbins.

"Above the trees," Zeb said. "A trail of lights will lead travelers to the delights of Centrum City's splendorous sights."

He reached and switched off the lantern, and the device quieted, dropping into his hands as he spoke in hushed tones.

"All our lands once sparkled wondrous. Dark times

came from selfish governors. As for Eb the Luminary, he reins from an old library."

Returning the lantern to a cabinet by the stove, Zeb waved his grandchildren from the room, and Grandma Betsy pushed up her glasses, turning to Zeb and thanking him for his kindness.

"We'll be leaving the car here," she said. "Our coach, that is. We'll simply need to gather a few provisions. I imagine a vehicle, even a disabled one, might be of more use to all of you than it is to us."

"You could use it as an outdoor refrigerator," Theodore said.

"In any case," Grandma Betsy said. "We do appreciate the hospitality."

Zeb, for his part, itched his bushy white mustache and nodded, taking the hint to retire into a back bedroom for the night. Grandma Betsy yawned as the door closed, and Theodore picked up Calipso, scratching under her chin and behind her ears.

"We have no idea where we are," he said.

His shoulders sagged, and tears welled in his eyes as his grandmother sat down beside him on the makeshift mattress of pillows and blankets.

"We aren't entirely lost," she said. "We know, at least, that we're in the land of the Boffins. And at any rate, I bet we're having a more interesting trip than your parents are. They're stuck in tourist traps while we have a whole new world to explore."

At the mention of Theodore's parents, he began to cry, for homesickness had set in; up to this point, he'd momentarily forgotten his mother playing volleyball at the rec center and his dad filling up the easy chair with Sunday farts, but now the reality of the situation became overwhelming, and even Calipso's purring was not enough to temper his sadness. He cried as he hadn't cried since he'd played catcher and a little league backswing had broken his nose.

"One day at a time," Grandma Betsy said.

She rubbed Theodore's shoulders until he fell asleep, both feeling the intensity that comes with the uncertainty of an unfamiliar place.

In the morning, Theodore woke to birds chirping outside the window while his grandmother laid out their provisions on the rug. They had a gallon of water, which it would be his job to carry, and an opened box of granola bars, two beef sticks, a wool blanket, and a first aid kit, not to mention the former governor's dusty boots, all of which Grandma Betsy would convey in the big cloth bag she'd used for grocery shopping.

Bowls of soup steamed, waiting on the windowsill.

"I've already spoken with Zeb," Grandma Betsy said. "The start of the lantern trail hangs above a clump of trees to the south."

"I'd rather not get out of bed," Theodore said.

"Theodore Maxwell Lyman," she said. "Come have a look."

She nudged his shoulder, looked him square in the eye, and winked.

"Zeb's given us a surprise," she said.

At this, Theodore did not feel quite so crestfallen, and he pulled on his long johns and pants and socks with a renewed sense of urgency, almost tripping as he stepped into his winter boots before buttoning his shirt.

"What kind of surprise?" he asked.

"It appears," Grandma Betsy said. "That Zeb and his daughter are fairly handy."

She lifted a blanket from the floor, and underneath, a backpack with air holes and a clear vinyl viewing port waited on the carpet.

"This way, we can bring Calipso with us," Grandma Betsy said.

Buttons secured the top flap, and inside, a thin board wrapped in flannel had been fitted to the bottom of the bag.

"They made us a cat carrier," Theodore said.

"It seems they're very happy we came along,"

Grandma Betsy said. "But we're also lucky we both brought hats and gloves and coats. This part of Um doesn't have paved roads. It'll be chilly."

Reinvigorated, Theodore slurped down his soup and finished dressing; he lowered Calipso into her new home, bribing her with a beef stick before buttoning the backpack and putting it on over his puffy coat. After picking up the water jug, he opened the dome's front door to a bright morning and found Boffin crews hard at work disassembling the fallen shed while another team patched the hole in the hillside fence. After saying goodbye to Zeb and thanking him profusely, Theodore and Grandma Betsy set off for Centrum City, grateful for clear skies as they picked up the lantern trail that was right where Zeb had said it would be.

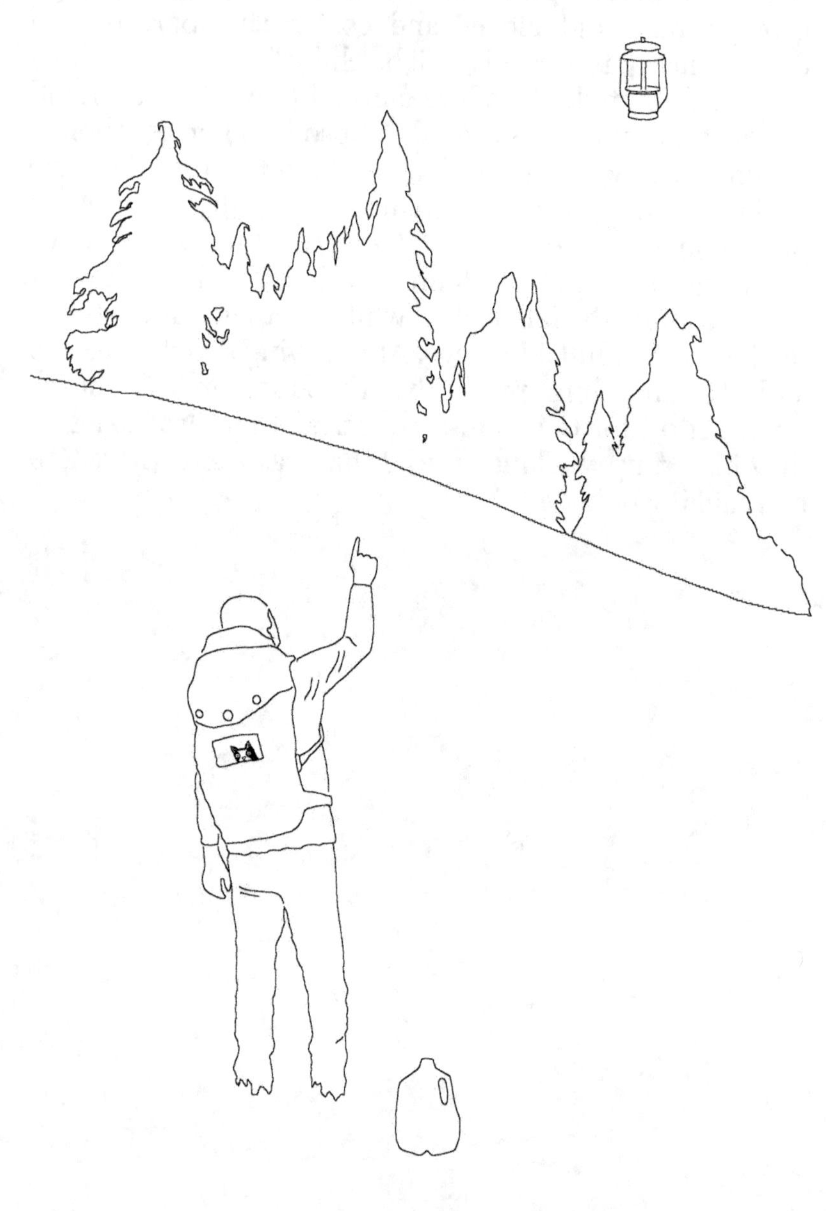

The Department Store Mannequin

From the looks of the landscape, the Boffins in the land of Um had suffered a mass evacuation or a cataclysm within recent decades. Here and there, rotten posts stuck up from untilled fields, and the few barns and dome houses Theodore and Grandma Betsy passed had the roofs caved in. Briar thickets ringed washed-out ditches. Shrubs had grown around rusted tractor rims. Clusters of evergreen trees dotted the rolling hills, but the countryside was mostly bare and ominously empty.

Thankfully, the guide lanterns floated 50 feet off the ground and were spaced out every half mile or so, glowing brightly enough that the line in either direction was easy to follow, and after several hours, they crossed a stone bridge that gave way to what had once been a little town with shops and a cobblestone plaza. Moss now covered most of the bricks, and ivy had climbed the cinder block walls, but storefront signs peeked through, here and there, block letters advertising gum and candies and refillable ink pens.

"Where do you think everyone went?" Theodore asked.

"I'd rather not guess," Grandma Betsy said. "But Zeb's people weren't worried about disease, so I suppose it wasn't a plague."

Most of the display windows had long-since been busted out, but many of the buildings still had shade beneath overhanging metal canopies, and Grandma Betsy sat down on a disintegrating boardwalk. She split a granola bar and handed half to Theodore.

"It's a ghost town," he said.

As he chewed and looked through the window frame at an old perfume counter sandwiched between display racks and a windblown menswear section, Theodore was surprised to see one of the pole-mounted display mannequins waving vigorously at him, its old suit in tatters, holes in the jacket.

"You," it said. "Yes, you."

"Who are you?" Theodore asked.

Grandma Betsy stood up and squinted, leaning towards the open window.

"We didn't think there was anyone here," she said.

The mannequin folded its hands behind its head, elbows out, as if reclining on a beach.

"Just a bunch of us dummies. Me and Burt and Geno and Shelley," he said. "But Shelley doesn't have a head. And Burt and Geno are both pretty quiet. I'm the talkative one."

"We don't want to bother you," Grandma Betsy said.

"Oh, it's no trouble at all. Nobody comes here, anymore. It's been years since I've had a chance to shoot the breeze."

Theodore set down his water jug and stepped up onto the boardwalk, testing the floor; Grandma Betsy held out a cautious hand before he ventured through the doorway.

"Why did they leave you behind?" she asked.

"Will you wait while I tell you?" it asked. "Please, do tell me if it's a story you've heard before."

"But we just met you," Theodore said.

"Ah, yes," the mannequin said. "But we have our own social circles, and word travels. For what it's worth, I came to be stationed here at the height of fashion, during the boom times, as they say."

The rack of bars that held the display in place must have been quite sturdy, as the broad gestures of the mannequin didn't cause any vibration whatsoever.

"I sold the ladies their dresses and the men their evening wear," it said. "I would chat with the mayor about the goings-on at city hall and model outfits for traveling performers. My banter was the talk of the town until everyone left. Governor Eyebright hasn't exactly been a patron of the arts, if you catch my drift."

"Where are you speaking from?" Theodore asked.

"Excuse me?"

Theodore had quietly walked between the clothing racks and stood immediately in front of the display.

"I don't see the microphone," Theodore said.

"I'm made entirely of lacquered oak, if that's what you're asking," the mannequin said. "Amazing that I haven't fallen prey to the elements. Or a woodpecker. Or termites."

"But you don't even have a face," Theodore said.

At this, the mannequin took offense, not because it thought Theodore was trying to be rude, but because its standards of beauty would not allow such a comment to go unchecked.

"I'll have you know," it said. "Mine is a look that is timeless. Styles come and go, but I allow the observer to imagine themselves in everything I wear."

"I can hear you, but I can't even tell where you're speaking from," Theodore said. "It doesn't seem like you have eyes or ears."

"Well," the mannequin said. "Aren't you a spunky young chap?"

"Are you happy the way you are?" Theodore asked.

"I wish I could say I was," the mannequin said. "But I had a falling out with the owner of this shop, and he's left me stuck in one place for what seems like ages."

Grandma Betsy, who had been leaning on the dusty perfume counter, blew on her hands, as the inside of the unheated store was no warmer than it was outside.

"What was your argument about?" she asked.

"Ah, that," the mannequin said. "He was irritated by my love of talk, my flattering and bantering and chattering. To him, it was all a shallow show of gossip. The rumor mill, he called it."

"You've clearly had some time to think," Grandma Betsy said.

"He always had his head stuck in a book," the mannequin said. "But after thousands of days of

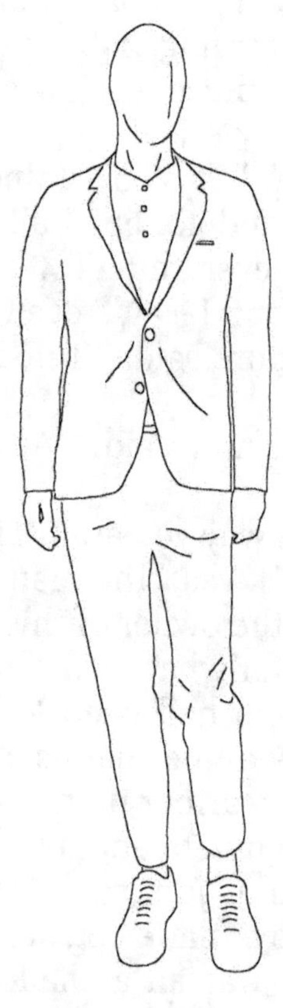

reflection, I've decided he might be on to something. Certainly, exercising the gift of gab is intoxicating, but I suspect there are deeper truths to be uncovered in tomes of literature."

"There is no friend as loyal as a book," Grandma Betsy said.

"Unfortunately," the mannequin said. "While I've had my sights set on the Centrum City library for some time, I'm likely a lost cause, for even if I were to travel there, staff would deny me entry, as people view a department store mannequin as a prop, rather than a person."

Fortunately for the mannequin, Grandma Betsy, who had an impulsive streak, was also a good judge of character, and it moved her to see anyone held back.

"My grandson and I seek an audience with the Luminary," she said. "Perhaps we can help each other."

"There will be dangers along the way," the mannequin said.

"Undoubtedly," Grandma Betsy said.

"And we'll encounter stranger things than talking displays," the mannequin said.

"Certainly," Grandma Betsy said.

Within minutes, Theodore found a screwdriver in a rusty can at the back of the shop and loosened the bolts that fixed the display in place. Having been lowered to the floor, the mannequin jumped and flexed and dusted itself off, glad to be free of the pole, and having promised Burt and Geno and Shelley that this would not be the last time they would meet, the mannequin strolled out the store's front door, gleefully pointing to the guide lantern that hung above the street lamps in the town square.

They Came Upon a Forest

While the mannequin may have aspired to radiate sage wisdom, it bounced and sang like a child as it walked over frozen farmland, delighted by the rising of the sun and the passing of unusual cloud shapes.

"That one reminds me of a griffin," the mannequin said.

"You have griffins here?" Theodore asked.

"I certainly hope not," the mannequin said. "I'd be terrified to meet one in the wild."

"Do you think they eat people?"

"Most certainly," the mannequin said. "But I'd gladly make a noble sacrifice of myself on your behalf."

"Let's hope it doesn't come to that," Grandma Betsy said.

And in this way, they continued on. Within a few hours, Grandma Betsy and Theodore grew accustomed to the constant chatter of their new friend and the distraction it provided from the desolate landscape with its caved-in barns and rusty silos. As it required no food and no sleep to fuel a seemingly limitless supply of endurance, the mannequin fascinated Theodore, as neither he nor his grandmother had ever met such a being in Wisconsin.

"But how were you created?" Theodore asked. "How does it all work?"

"To my knowledge," the mannequin said. "I was fashioned by craftsmen who had a shop adjacent to a sawmill in the outskirts of Centrum City. Once they'd routed out my arms and legs and joints and screwed everything together, I was put in a box and mailed to the shop you found me in."

"He means," Grandma Betsy said. "How are you animated? What gives you the energy to move?"

At this, the mannequin shrugged.

"I could ask the same of you," it said. "What makes your legs and arms and eyes and ears keep working?"

"We," Theodore said. "Have brains that send messages down nerves in our arms, and the messages tell muscles to move or take signals from our eyes and ears back to our brains. We have hearts that pump blood throughout our bodies to make sure our organs have everything they need to keep operating."

"That is what makes you alive?" the mannequin asked.

They had come upon hilly terrain, and as the land grew steep and rocky, ash and maple and poplar trees grew from the slopes.

"No, I guess dead people have blood and brains and hearts, at least for a little while," Theodore said.

"Then what," the mannequin asked. "Would you say makes you alive? Why only people and cats and things with certain kinds of face holes?"

"In my experience," Grandma Betsy said. "Things that are alive only come from other things that are alive."

"But they have made test tube babies," Theodore said.

Snowy trails wound their way past fallen fences and broken granite chunks, everything separated by brush with bare branches that grew thick and untamed.

"I suppose," Grandma Betsy said. "There has to be a spark of life for something to be alive, and when it leaves, the body falls limp like a puppet without its strings."

"If that is the case, then I must have a spark of life just as you have a spark of life," the mannequin said. "Although I honestly have no idea where I got it."

"You don't remember anything?" Theodore asked. "What is your earliest memory?"

"I remember being in the box on the way to the store I worked in," the mannequin said. "I remember being in the woodworker shop and climbing into a box of packing peanuts. I remember my shoulder joints being slotted into my chest cavity and the arm bolts tightening down."

Of the three, Grandma Betsy moved the slowest along the overgrown bluff, bracing herself on rocks as she climbed with Theodore, who scampered after the mannequin. Throughout the day, the air had grown chillier, and Grandma Betsy knew how important it would be to find warm shelter before nightfall, along with food to carry them through. It was hard going, at least for the humans, as their feet sunk into the snow. Lanterns twinkled above, and by late afternoon, they had reached the top of the ridge, which overlooked an enormous valley.

"The governors of the different parts of Um have very different reputations," the mannequin said. "Governor Eyebright can see through walls and liquefy people with a glance."

"Could," Theodore said.

"Could?" the mannequin asked.

"He's deceased."

"Well," the mannequin said. "That's a relief."

"Do you see the smoke?" Grandma Betsy asked.

She pointed, and past towering oaks and verdant pines, nestled between a pond and the eroding hillside, white wisps trailed from the chimney of a cabin.

"We'll be needing a place to rest," she said.

"Speak for yourself," the mannequin said.

Ducks flew overhead, a flock rising above snowy branches as Grandma Betsy and Theodore and the mannequin made their way along a deer trail towards the white plume of chimney smoke.

"We're coming to Centrum City from the north," the mannequin said. "Each region has its own season. Here, there are long winters. In the south, it's usually summer. To the east, a long spring awaits, whereas the west enjoys a long, dark descent into fall."

As they followed the downward curve of the valley wall, broken chunks of slate and ice-covered tree roots impeded progress. Shrubs grew between boulders, life clinging to stony soil, and Grandma Betsy held onto saplings to keep her footing.

"Most of the governors were appointed long before the

Luminary arrived," the mannequin said. "So unless things have changed, Governor Goldfinch is the governor of lies and truths and can transmute anything, especially people, into gold. Governor Cloverfield has the wings of an enormous bat and brings youth to the elderly or age to the youngsters, and Governor Mourningdove is an oracle who can turn people invisible."

"And the Luminary?" Grandma Betsy asked.

"Before his arrival," the mannequin said. "Centrum City was a small village circled around the Tree of Life that grows in the middle of Um. Despite the corruption of the governors, the Luminary's turned a tiny hamlet into a modern metropolis, a place of beauty and awe."

Theodore was the first to reach the valley floor, and he paused to take off his backpack. He unbuttoned the top and swapped his water jug for Calipso, who had been fast asleep in the bottom of the bag. Ahead, beyond the frozen pond, the cabin waited, smoke drifting from its chimney, thick walls made from rough-hewn logs, icicles hanging from shingle edges, everything framing a red front door that to Theodore was almost begging to be knocked.

Sublime Industries Unit D1

A robot with gleaming blue eyes vacuumed in the living room as Grandma Betsy waved from the open doorway.

"Visitors!" it said. "Welcome! As a Sublime D1 series unit, I'm at your disposal."

The motor quieted, and the droid's arm extended, telescoping to pluck the vacuum's plug from the wall socket. To the left of the door, velvet-upholstered settees provided ample seating, flanked by end tables and high-backed wooden chairs.

"Please," the D1 said. "Do come in. Would anyone like a beverage? I fear the crackers may have fallen to dust in their boxes, but I certainly have tea."

"I'd like tea," Theodore said.

"Would you like us to take off our shoes?" Grandma Betsy asked.

"I don't believe I'd be able to drink tea," the mannequin said.

"Lovely," the D1 said. "Yes, please, set your shoes on the slatted wooden shelf to your right and then make yourselves at home. I imagine you'll need to warm up, if you came on foot."

"We hope we're not intruding," Grandma Betsy said. "We've been following the trail of lanterns, and it's led us to your valley."

"Who else lives here?" Theodore asked.

Wrapping the vacuum cord, the robot made a sighing sound, long limbs retracting, blue eyes dimming.

"You aren't highwaymen, are you?" it asked.

"What are highwaymen?" Theodore asked.

"Scoundrels," the D1 said. "Robbers. Outlaws. Bandits."

"Certainly not," Grandma Betsy said. "We've traveled here, quite by accident, from Wisconsin, and we're on our way to the Luminary in Centrum City."

"And I, for my part," the mannequin said. "Look to immerse myself in literature, as allowed by the librarians at the main branch."

At this, the robot brightened, and it stowed its vacuum in a small cupboard before extruding its arm to press the switch on an electric kettle.

"Thank you for your clarification," it said. "I've been alone for an extended period, having cared for Mr. Zeke Glum, the former owner of this cabin, until his death due to old age some two years ago. He was a private man, and we seldom had visitors."

The kettle rumbled, and bubbling rose to a rolling boil before the button clicked off; by that time, the robot had set two porcelain teacups on a tray, along with an assortment of tea bags from a tin box. Theodore pulled the door shut and set down Calipso, whom he had been holding close to his chest.

"I'm sorry for your loss," Grandma Betsy said.

"I'm glad I can be a host, for once," the D1 said.

"Besides the tea, do you have any food?" Grandma Betsy asked. "Anything edible?"

Shoes discarded, the mannequin sat himself on an ottoman and kicked his feet back and forth; Grandma Betsy and Theodore unzipped their coats, hanging their gloves and hats on wall pegs. Heat radiated from the wood stove in the corner, logs visible through tinted isinglass, and the robot left the tray with its steaming cups on a coffee table in the center of the room.

"We have some canned fish and jars of vegetables in the larder," the D1 said. "You're welcome to help yourselves. It was Mr. Glum's dying request that I keep the house turnkey ready, and as I'm obligated to carry out the nonviolent wishes of everyone I happen across, I've been maintaining the residence day and night."

"In what way," Grandma Betsy asked. "Are you obligated?"

"Sublime units are programmed to help anyone they see and never hurt a living thing," the D1 said.

"Its series was decommissioned 30 years ago," the mannequin said. "They tend to get stuck in loops."

"How do you mean stuck in loops?" Theodore asked.

While Grandma Betsy warmed her hands by the stove, Calipso circled Theodore's legs, her black tail flitting against an iron poker that hung from the wall with a small metal shovel and a broom.

"If memory serves, some glitched out and scrubbed holes in the floor," the mannequin said. "They'd lay shingles over shingles and trim hedges until there was nothing left. I'm surprised to see one in operation."

The robot's eyes flickered as the mannequin spoke, and a low groan pulsed from its mesh speaker.

"I believe," the D1 said. "Reports of malfunctions have been overstated."

"I hope we're not making you unhappy," Grandma Betsy said. "We're grateful to find you here after a long day walking through fields. Indebted, really."

"May I speak freely?" the D1 asked.

Theodore ripped the top from a tea packet, and, sniffing the strong scent of orange peelings and cinnamon, dunked the bag in his cup. The mannequin, spotting a book under a reading lamp, flipped on the light and turned to the first page. The robot, sensing the needs of Calipso, filled a dish with water and set it on the floor.

"You've taken us in from the cold," Grandma Betsy said. "Listening to your thoughts is the least we can do."

"You're too kind," the D1 said. "In any case, the mannequin is, in general, correct. My series of droids do sometimes get stuck and repeat ourselves. As a larger concern, we have very little agency, due to our programming. Of course, I take no issue with the first directive that forbids me from causing pain or harm to humanoid creatures."

"Naturally," Grandma Betsy said.

"But the second rule, that I must provide for each and every person who gives me an instruction, means that I have little control over my own destiny," it said. "Mr.

Glum told me to take care of this house, and I have been compelled to do so ever since, regardless of isolation or monotony or my own goals."

"What would you rather be doing?" Grandma Betsy asked.

Producing a canister of oil-packed cod from the pantry, the robot pulled the tab and peeled back the top lid.

"I think," it said. "I'd like to travel and see the places that were so precisely coded into my matrix."

Fish spread across a small plate, the robot left it next to the water dish, and Calipso quickly scarfed down her food, purring as she ate.

"If you would like," Grandma Betsy said. "You could accompany us as we travel to Centrum City."

The robot's eyes flashed, and it held up a single finger.

"One problem will undoubtedly arise," it said. "As I've noted, I'm compelled to help anyone who requests my aid, and as such, I might wander off at a moment's notice."

Theodore cupped his tea, blowing before sipping.

"Then we'll have to make sure that doesn't happen," he said.

"Hopefully, we can find someone who can update your programming," Grandma Betsy said. "And then you can be the architect of your own fate."

With this, everyone settled in for the evening. Grandma Betsy and Theodore and Calipso quickly fell asleep beneath warm blankets as the mannequin read and the robot prepared the house for what it imagined would be a long absence.

Fowl and Unseen

In the morning, after the D1 robot finished shuttering the cabin, everyone set off for Centrum City. Glowing lanterns lit up a gray sky, clouds having rolled in from the west; despite the overcast weather, full stomachs kept Grandma Betsy and Theodore and Calipso in high spirits, with the boy running ahead and whacking trees with sticks while his grandmother whistled and marveled at the enormous mushrooms that grew from the trunks and branches of towering oaks. Up the side of the valley wall, pine boughs brushed the floorboards of a rusty chairlift that swayed with the wind, a relic from a long-defunct ski resort.

"Visitors flocked to the slopes on the weekends," the D1 said.

"This used to be a tourist trap?" Grandma Betsy asked.

"That's what led Mr. Glum to settle here," the D1 said. "For many years, he was the owner and proprietor of Glum Mountain, a location famous for fresh powder on groomed trails. Initially, he brought me in as a handyman doing repair work on suspended drive motors, although I dabbled in groundskeeping and lodge maintenance."

"A jack of all trades," Grandma Betsy said.

"As it were," the D1 said. "There was less fear of me falling or being harassed by invisible turkeys than my flesh-in-blood counterparts. Did you know an aerial tramway once ran with the lantern trail to Centrum City?"

"Invisible turkeys?" Grandma Betsy asked.

"Many years ago, when Governor Mourningdove paid a visit to the region, Mr. Glum earned her ire by honoring Governor Eyebright's already-existing reservation of the penthouse suite," the D1 said. "Mourningdove responded by releasing hundreds of translucent game birds to attack people for miles around. Facing lawsuits and mounting debts, Mr. Glum sold the resort and became a recluse."

"That's terrible," Grandma Betsy said.

"It certainly wasn't a walk in the park," the D1 said.

"Or a donkey ride to heaven," Grandma Betsy said.

Carried by the wind, thick, white flakes swirled around pine trees, falling past ice-encrusted limbs that sagged, heavy with snow.

"How'd you get rid of the turkeys?" Theodore asked.

"We didn't," the D1 said. "They've been a blight on the landscape for years. Occasionally, they peck an unsuspecting traveler within an inch of his life."

"So we should stay alert," Grandma Betsy said.

"Should we face an attack," the mannequin said. "I'll yell and draw them off. After all, beyond ripping holes in my clothes, there isn't much they can do to me."

"And I," the D1 said. "Can strobe my floodlights while extending my limbs to make myself appear very large."

Stopping at a fallen log, Grandma Betsy took a jar of vegetable soup from her bag and unscrewed the top.

"The further we go along," she said. "The more this seems like a place children would dream about."

"You aren't entirely wrong," the mannequin said.

"How so?" she asked.

"Last night," the mannequin said. "I read the book Mr. Glum generously left behind on the history of Um, a book both interesting and illuminating, given our current situation."

Grandma Betsy passed the soup to Theodore, who had taken off his backpack to check on Calipso, who was fast asleep and purring softly.

"And?" Theodore asked.

The mannequin, who still relished its recent emancipation from the crumbling department store, leaned on a knothole, unaffected by the cold and the wind that had brought redness to Theodore's nose and cheeks.

"The text was dense," the mannequin said. "But it claimed Um is adjacent to many worlds and has had many visitors over countless eons. The Boffins came hundreds of thousands of years ago, as did the Zards and the Trogs, along with humans and elves. But the elves have been here the longest."

"Elves?" Grandma Betsy asked.

"Apparently," the mannequin said. "Only very specific conditions allow people to slip between dimensions."

"What kinds of conditions?" Grandma Betsy asked.

Theodore drank soup in a giant slurp, then handed the jar back to his grandmother, who replaced the lid.

"The book was more about concepts," the mannequin said. "It didn't explain the mechanics in great detail."

"I see," Grandma Betsy said.

"But it did say that a good many intelligent creatures have visions of worlds beyond their own in nightmares or moments of woolgathering."

"Woolgathering?" Theodore asked.

"Daydreaming," the D1 said.

"Again, you mentioned elves?" Grandma Betsy asked.

The mannequin folded its hands behind its head and sighed.

"Oh, yes," it said. "All of our recent governors have been elves. They aren't devious by nature, but it seems that the devious ones are the few who rise to power."

"Devious elves," Theodore said. "Good to know."

The robot made a clicking sound and held up a finger. Wind whistled through the trees, and white noise had filled the valley.

"While the turkeys don't reflect light," the D1 said. "They aren't quiet, and there's a great deal of noise headed our way. Thankfully, I believe I have a solution, if you'll indulge me."

"Please," Grandma Betsy said.

Gears humming, the robot took her by the waist and grew taller, its legs extruding as it lifted Grandma Betsy to the branches of an oak some 20 feet from the ground.

"Sit tight," it said.

It returned for Theodore and raised him to a

neighboring treetop, winking as it left him clinging to the trunk, backpack in hand.

"Don't worry," the D1 said. "We got this."

And then it lowered itself and was quickly lost in a blizzard of gobbling and flapping and yelling and bright lights.

Something Big Is in the Woods

For over an hour, Grandma Betsy and Theodore clung to the trunks of their respective trees, waiting. Occasionally, nearby twigs snapped or yelps met with the beating of wings, but from the high-up perches, it was hard to see anything besides the shine of the D1 robot's eyes as it strode past, whipping its arms about. Occasionally, the mannequin ran beneath the tree, bellowing and kicking, but the wind and the invisible turkeys kicked up enough snow to obscure the view, resulting in ground cover that looked like TV static.

"We'll have some good stories to tell," Grandma Betsy yelled. "Won't we?"

"I don't think anyone will believe us," Theodore yelled.

Gradually, the powdery haze settled, and the robot appeared on stilt legs, peering through the branches.

"I believe," it said. "We've taken the wind out of their sails and chased them off. Turkey Toms can be quite aggressive, but they got more than they'd bargained for."

Hugging Theodore and his backpack, the robot lowered itself to a forest floor littered with broken limbs and pine needles and dented snow drifts before it rose again to retrieve Grandma Betsy. The mannequin sat on a stump, having taken off its suit jacket to inspect the large rip that ran down the back.

"Savage creatures," it said. "Not that I've had plans to present myself as a runway model in the near future, but I can certainly see why the resort lost its customers."

"It would've been horrible if my grandma and I were out here on our own," Theodore said.

"Thankfully," the D1 said. "You weren't."

With Grandma Betsy's feet firmly on the ground, the robot's limbs shrank until it was no taller than a sapling. Theodore, who had unbuttoned the backpack to feed

Calipso a small piece of ham, picked up his water jug and twisted off the cap for a drink.

"It looks like it was quite the skirmish," Grandma Betsy said.

"One thing that works against the turkeys," the D1 said. "Is that they can't see each other and collide when conflict arises, trampling and screeching and causing chaos. Having lived in the woods for a good long while, I've learned to anticipate their antics."

Bending, the mannequin picked up a half-buried pine cone.

"Aside from my jacket getting caught and ripped, I have to say I found the tussle rather liberating," it said. "A few pecks and collisions, but no real damage done."

"A bit of life experience," Grandma Betsy said. "I know my poetry really took off once I'd traveled and seen a bit more of the world."

As Theodore secured his backpack, the robot took a moment to listen to the stillness of the valley, and within minutes, the group again set out on the path that wound its way through the woods.

"I didn't know you wrote poems," Theodore said.

"You learn something new every day," Grandma Betsy said. "So long as you're paying attention."

By noon, the forest had grown thick, and had it not been for the robot's floodlight eyes, Theodore wouldn't have been able to see his hand in front of his face. Evergreen trees grew close together, so close, in fact, that the snow had scarcely reached the ground, and everyone walked on a bed of pine needles several inches thick. Three-tailed raccoons scampered from holes in rotten stumps and peeked around mossy rocks, their beady yellow eyes glinting in the shadows.

"I'll keep us on a southerly course," the D1 said. "I had no idea the land had become so overgrown. I expect we're near the edge of the valley, but it's hard to say, as this whole area was grasslands 40 years ago."

"Perhaps," Grandma Betsy said. "You should poke

your head up through the canopy."

"You're sure young Mr. Theodore wouldn't be frightened by the darkness?" the D1 asked.

"Not at all," Theodore said. "Not for a minute."

So the robot's legs again lengthened, and the light faded from the understory as the droid rose through pine boughs to the treetops.

"It's like being in a cave," Theodore said.

"It'll only be a minute," Grandma Betsy said.

Holding hands in the gloom, Theodore and Grandma Betsy and the mannequin listened to the hoot of an owl. Water trickled somewhere in the inky murkiness, the sound of a stream rushing over hidden rocks.

"Excuse me," a low voice said. "You're standing on my foot."

"Pardon?" Grandma Betsy asked.

"My foot," the voice said. "If you could please move, you're standing right on my toe."

"Who, me?" Theodore asked.

"Everyone, move," the mannequin said.

After a great deal of shuffling and inching forward, a sigh of relief breathed from the blackness.

"I found my way to the deepest part of the forest, and still I run into people," it said. "Apparently, there's no escaping the reach of Governor Eyebright and his legions of spies."

By now, the robot had begun its descent back through the evergreen boughs, but going was slow, and the glow from his eyes had yet to pierce the needles and illuminate the forest floor.

"I'll have you know, Governor Eyebright is dead," Grandma Betsy said. "And none of us are spies. Quite the opposite."

"We're trying to get back to Wisconsin," Theodore said.

"Then you've brought good news," the voice said. "At least until someone puts an even worse person in charge of things."

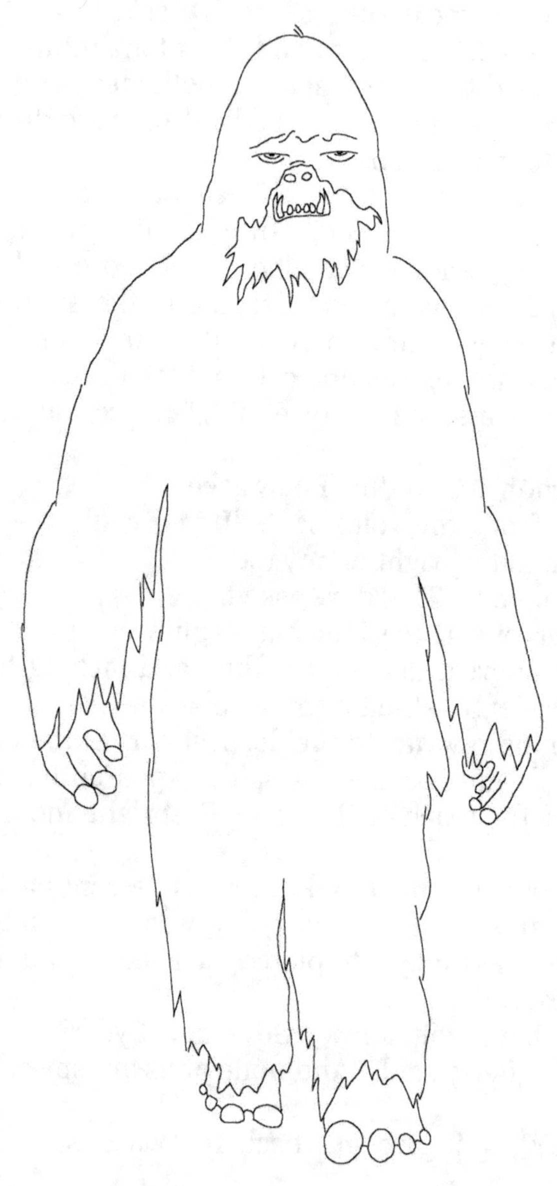

The voice moved, and a mountain of fur stepped into the growing light. Theodore first thought the creature looked something like a wookiee, tall and shaggy, a walking fur coat easily nine feet tall. The creature shifted its weight, shielding its eyes with enormous hands that terminated in rock-like finger pads, before stepping sideways with feet the size of snowshoes.

"You're Bigfoot," Theodore said.

"My name's Gary," the bigfoot said.

The robot reached ground level, and his eye beams swept across Gary's red-brown fur, and the stump with the three-tailed raccoons, and an abandoned wagon that had nearly been subsumed by weeds, then back to the toothy maw and bulbous nose beneath Gary's forehead crest.

"Gary," Grandma Betsy said. "Meet the D1 robot, the mannequin, and my grandson, Theodore. We have a pet cat sleeping in the backpack, as well, and we're on our way to Centrum City."

"A cat," Gary said. "I love cats."

Dimming its floodlights, the robot scanned the brush, beams focusing on a narrow corridor of light past a rocky outcrop.

"We're close to the trail lantern," the D1 said. "The dirt road has all but disappeared."

The ground shook slightly as Gary turned and waved for everyone to follow, stepping over a rotting log covered in toadstools.

"One way or another, you found me," he said. "The least I can do is get you out of the cold for a nice lunch."

And with that, everyone followed Gary through the woods and along a small stream to an old barn filled with antiques the bigfoot had collected during his quiet travels. They did so without a second thought, because the eyes of the sasquatch shone with kindness, vibrating on a frequency that resonated across all forms of life.

Grandma Betsy and Theodore ladled soup from a drum hung over the barn's makeshift fireplace. Duct work ran up the wall from the stone hearth, and Gary cooked mushrooms with onions in an iron skillet.

"You have a lovely home," Grandma Betsy said.

"Something smells like wet socks," Theodore said.

"Theodore Maxwell," Grandma Betsy said.

"No," Gary said. "He's right. I've been letting things go."

Bags of potting soil sat with seed trays on a picnic table, and baskets of yarn filled an old feed bin. Planks between stacked cinder blocks served as shelves supporting sacks of potatoes and a canister of wax cylinders and a huge glass jar filled with deer antlers.

"I always mean to get out more," Gary said. "It's easy to fall into a loop of self-isolation."

"After Frank's funeral, I didn't leave the house for over a month," Grandma Betsy said.

"Who's Frank?" Gary asked.

"My husband," Grandma Betsy said.

"I'm sorry for your loss," Gary said.

Not knowing what to do with itself, the D1 robot tugged clumps of moss from the walls, which it laid in a wheelbarrow near the barn's sliding door. The mannequin, who professed a dislike for open flames, stayed as far away from the hearth as possible, opting to pick through boxes of knickknacks on metal racks. Old mining helmets were stacked on a crate filled with rusty hatchets alongside a bullet press. A nearby wooden cabinet had built-in speakers and opened to reveal an ancient radio with a ruby diode as its core.

"You're cultivating quite the curiosity shop," the mannequin said.

"Take anything you like," Gary said. "I try to rescue

lost possessions. Since the woods have spread and folks migrated to the city, I've found hundreds of abandoned houses filled with treasure."

Windup soldiers peeked from tin canisters; an enormous studded leather jacket hung from a wall hook. Porcelain tea sets occupied a violin case. A cooler held a camping tent and its folded poles; cigar boxes and a bronze telescope had fallen against the torso of a Sublime B3 automaton.

"I've found your cousin," the mannequin said. "At least, partially."

"Most of my cousins died in the chaos that predated the rule of the governors," Gary said.

"My cousins live in Nebraska," Grandma Betsy said.

"Mikey and Pat live in Milwaukee," Theodore said.

"Not you," the mannequin said. "I'm talking to the D1."

Pausing, perhaps for emotional emphasis, the mannequin waited for everyone to turn before it wiped a thick layer of dust from the shoulder of the headless and limbless B3 unit, and this gesture, small yet deliberate, triggered a series of clicks from the D1 robot, who immediately left the wheelbarrow it had been filling with moss and stepped over a kerosene lamp to better scrutinize the remains of the dismembered mechanoid.

"Wires have been sheared off," the D1 said. "It appears it was torn apart."

"If you're up for a challenge," Gary said. "There're more pieces in the storage closet, although I confess they're in even worse condition than the torso. I found the automaton strewn around the base of the Wandering Cliffs to the west and assumed it had fallen before being attacked by animals."

"B3s were almost exclusively used for land surveys and timber felling," the D1 robot said. "There're likely dozens still wandering through Boffin lands looking for trees to chop down."

Grandma Betsy blew on the surface of her potato-dumpling soup as the D1 disappeared into a small room under the loft's overhang. Theodore, having already burned his tongue on a hot spoonful, sat on an over-sized foot stool waiting for his bowl to cool.

"What're the Wandering Cliffs?" Grandma Betsy asked.

Gary scooped onions and mushrooms onto a small platter before leaving his skillet to soak in a bucket of water.

"The topography of Um isn't entirely fixed," he said. "There're cliffs that meander through the forest, never staying in one place. My parents thought they moved when nobody was watching."

The D1 robot carried a trunk out from the storage area and set it beside the B3 unit's torso. The hand on the left arm had two remaining fingers and a thumb, while the right hand was fairly intact beneath a considerably bent hydraulic piston. Both legs had severe gnaw marks, especially where they had been wrenched away from the main body, as did the upper limbs near the shoulder. The head, which resembled ski goggles on a batting helmet, included cracked eyes and a mouthpiece that no longer stayed in its socket.

"He's a bit worse for wear," Gary said. "I didn't want to do more damage by tinkering with things I'm not qualified to fix."

"For what it's worth," the mannequin said. "You've certainly found troves of lost treasures."

The D1 robot gently set the B3's limbs down like the bones of a skeleton, such that it could be seen as a whole body. Tattered chrome ribbons failed to conceal gears and servos; deformed steel bore a faded Sublime Industries stamp. Calipso, whom Theodore had let out of the backpack, wound her way around the deactivated droid, her tail gently flicking across grimy metal.

"My larger concern," Gary said. "Is that nobody has been maintaining the infrastructure out here. Filled with antiques or not, many of the abandoned homes and buildings are packed with toxic substances that poison the forest. Defective trail lanterns fall from the treetops and cause fires before they're replaced."

Soup having cooled, Grandma Betsy ate a dumpling, then set her spoon in her bowl.

"Thus far," she said. "As fresh visitors to Um, we've not crossed paths with anyone truly evil."

"Although we did hit someone with our car," Theodore said.

"What I'm saying," she said. "Is that everyone we've met has been polite, with the exception of the invisible turkeys."

"But those were birds," Theodore said.

The mannequin pulled a bicycle from a stack of tarps, the rubber wheels having gone flat, the chain stiffened by rust.

"I've found that people are usually polite everywhere," Gary said. "When they aren't under the spell of an ancient evil."

Calipso rubbed up against Gary's leg, purring, and he set down a chunk of fish for her.

"Maybe," Grandma Betsy said. "You can kill two birds with one stone."

"I do enjoy eating birds," Gary said.

"She means," Theodore said. "You can do two things at once."

"Go on," Gary said.

Fingers tented, Grandma Betsy leaned on a wooden workbench.

"Until the powers that be install a new governor," she said. "Who controls the region?"

Gary ate an onion and wrinkled his thick brow in thought. After a moment, he tapped his spoon on the edge of the soup pot.

"While the elves have a historical claim to Um," he said. "Much of the population has fled to Centrum City, and the Luminary serves as the de facto ruler. I suppose he's as much in control as anyone."

Theodore chewed a potato and set down his bowl before picking up Calipso, who, having finished her snack, purred and closed her eyes.

"May I go out on a limb and say you enjoy the company of nice people?" Grandma Betsy asked.

"Indeed, I've been quite lonely," Gary said.

"And would you agree that a good many people would enjoy the curiosities of the forest?" Grandma Betsy asked.

"Even if it smells like old socks," Theodore said.

Gary ran a rock-fingered paw through his thick mane and stood, leaning against the hearth.

"You're saying I should go see the Luminary," he said. "And set myself up as a destination location."

"Seems like a good idea to me," Grandma Betsy said.

"And what," Gary asked. "What shall I do if I draw the interest of a new governor who is worse than Eyebright?"

"I suppose it's up to any of us to decide whether to act," Grandma Betsy said. "Or sit on our hands."

Gary ate a forkful of onions and smiled a huge, snaggle-toothed grin, aware for the first time in a long time that a plan was unfolding.

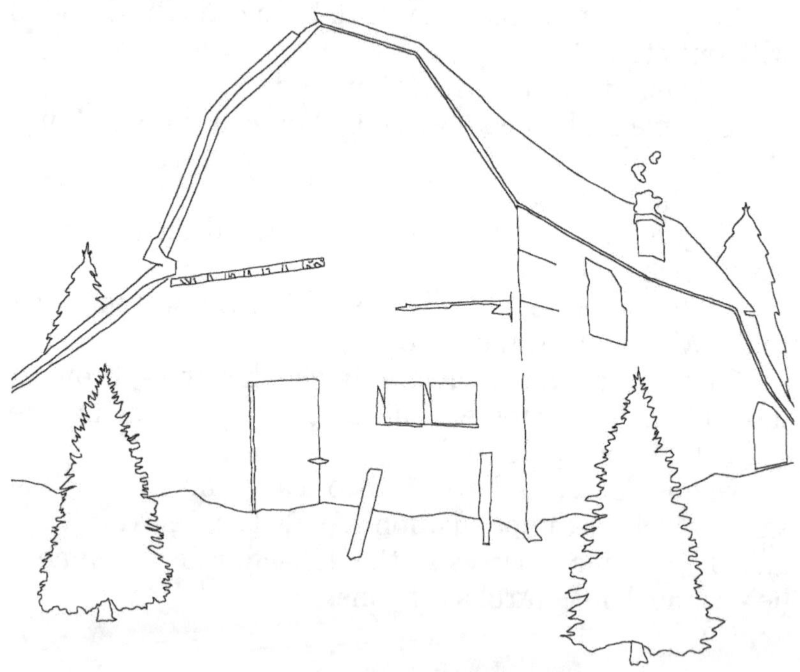

Towards the Outer Ring

After filling mason jars with soup and tightening down widemouthed lids, Gary agreed to tag along and seek an audience with the Grand Luminary.

"We're half a day's walk from the edge of the Ring," he said.

"The Ring?" Grandma Betsy asked.

The D1 robot, who had been uncoiling snapped cables from the neck hole of the B3 automaton, reached to pluck needle-nosed pliers from a tool pouch that hung from a pegboard hook.

"A giant wall surrounds Centrum City," the D1 said. "It was new when I initially booted up."

"The ring was constructed," the mannequin said. "By the Luminary's first crop of droids. The metropolis became a magnet attracting people from everywhere across Um."

Working quietly, Gary packed the jars of soup, along with a bag of onions and two dozen cloves of garlic, into a wooden crate that had been fitted with backpack straps.

"The governors each have castles in their fiefdoms," the mannequin said. "For unknown reasons, when the Luminary came along, the elven council ceded him the very center of Um, and Centrum City sprung up almost overnight."

"He's a figure of much speculation," Gary said.

"I actually saw him once," the D1 said. "On the day of my creation, one of the first things I did before being sold off to Mr. Glum for ski resort work was to take part in some kind of parade. My group was composed entirely of like-minded units, and we walked in rows and columns to the Tree of Life."

The mannequin held the B3 unit steady while the D1 connected an adapter to its pinkie finger before reaching deep within the chest cavity. Across the room, after slipping his arms through nylon backpack straps, Gary stood up with the wooden crate on his back.

"And?" Theodore asked.

"And what?" the D1 asked.

"What's the rest of the story?" Theodore asked. "Tell us about the time you saw the Luminary."

With its arm up to the elbow in the B3 unit, the D1 gave a sudden shudder. Its eyes dimmed momentarily, and a fan inside the old torso kicked on, blowing out dusty air.

"I remember," the D1 said. "That we stood still for a long time while the elves arrived. The Luminary told an elderly elf that the army had been instructed to cut down the tree, should he ever be killed. They discussed territories on a map for about four minutes, and then the procession marched to the Sublime Industries plaza, which is where I met Mr. Glum."

"That doesn't quite sound like a parade," Grandma Betsy said.

"Wait," Theodore said. "Is the Luminary an elf?"

Muffled clicks came from the B3 torso, and lights flickered in its abdomen. Motors whined, and ticking sounds came from gating modules.

"You don't know?" the mannequin asked.

"Don't know what?" Theodore asked.

"The Luminary's a human," the mannequin said. "Or at least he appears as one."

"Why do you think we all speak English?" Gary asked.

"I hadn't even thought about it," Theodore said.

Brightness returned to the D1 unit's eyes, and it withdrew its hand from the dismembered B3 robot.

"By all accounts, the Luminary is a force to be reckoned with," it said. "Incidentally, your conclusions were correct, Gary. The B3 was caught in the advancing ground swell of the Wandering Cliffs while running diagnostics on itself. The unit's playback, before runtime suspended, shows a troll tearing it limb from limb."

"A troll!" Grandma Betsy exclaimed. "Goodness!"

"Indeed," Gary said. "They're all but extinct."

Theodore returned Calipso to the backpack, and Grandma Betsy helped pack the B3 unit into boxes.

"While connected to the droid," the D1 said. "I ran a scan and compiled a list of repair tasks required to restore my comrade to working order. Unfortunately, it's a very long list."

"You're a good egg," Grandma Betsy said.

"An egg?" the D1 asked.

"You take care of those in need," she said.

"It's in my programming," the D1 said.

Gary, with the wooden crate on his back, pulled open the barn door, and within minutes, the group reached the treeline and was trudging through open fields. Trail lanterns sparkled in the cloudy sky, and decaying wooden rails from leaning fences littered the landscape. Much as the countryside near Zeb's geodesic dome community had been punctuated by occasional ramshackle houses, so did gutted cabins and cottages accent the emptiness of the wintry meadows.

Grandma Betsy walked with the robot, cloth bag swaying on her arm as the two led the way through ankle-deep snow. Theodore and the mannequin dawdled behind, kicking ice chunks and rocks that poked up from drifts, and Gary stayed between the two duos, listening and chiming in with the wisdom of a seasoned wallflower.

"When we got here, we met Boffins," Theodore said. "But we haven't seen any Zards or Trogs."

"There's a reason for that," the mannequin said. "The Zards are a scaly, reptilian people from a desert world that orbits worryingly close to a bright star, and for ease of comfort, they've settled the sun-baked lands to the south."

"They live by a strict code of honor," Gary said.

Glass soup jars clinked in Gary's crate, and the mannequin side-armed a sandstone chunk at a rusty pole that had nearly been pushed sideways by persistent pine saplings.

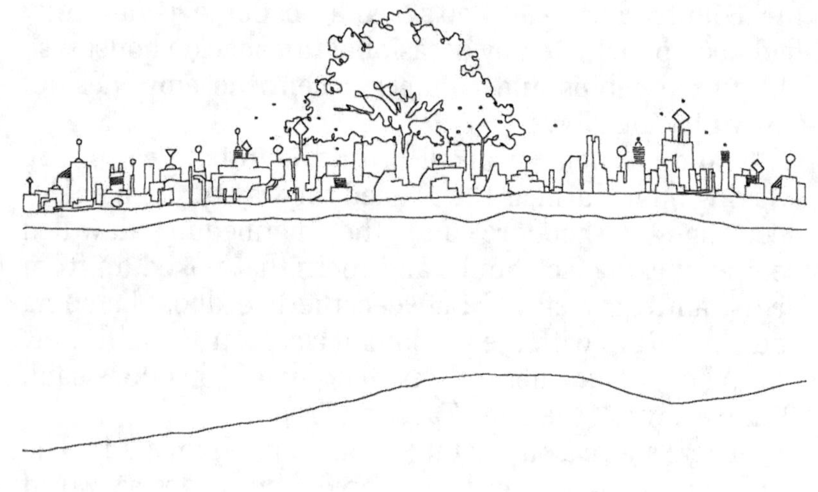

"The Trogs, in the east, are a clannish people fixated on games of sport," the mannequin said. "It's hard to miss forehead horns."

Theodore bent to pick up a flat skipping stone, and in the distance, following the bend of the horizon, a gray line curved beneath jagged teeth that reached up into glowing clouds. Above the Centrum City skyline, lights twinkled in the firmament, luminescence shimmering above the sprawling metropolis.

"Who lives in the west?" Theodore asked.

"Come again?" the mannequin asked.

"We met Boffins in the north, and you say there are Zards in the south and Trogs to the east," Theodore said. "But who lives west of here?"

He pocketed his stone and noted that the snow had turned to slush, nearly soaking his shoes, with green shoots poking up through muddy sludge.

"The west," Gary said. "Is the stronghold of the elves, and they view the other lands as colonies."

"If you look," the mannequin said. "You can see floating barges docking at skyspires."

Theodore slogged ahead, peering at gleaming distant towers surrounded by ships that zipped about like bees going about hive business.

"How do we know we'll get in to see him?" Theodore asked.

"Who?" the mannequin asked.

"The Luminary," Theodore said. "Who else?"

Pausing to roll up its soaked pants cuffs, the mannequin brushed melting ice chunks from its socks.

"Ah, well," it said. "I don't think you have to worry about that."

"It's a big city," Theodore said. "He probably deals with lots of people."

"The thing is," the mannequin said. "You and your grandmother are human, and unless things have changed a great deal around here, humans are very, very rare."

The Gates of Centrum City

Up close, Theodore guessed that the wall surrounding the city was at least as tall as a five-story building. Smooth like tempered glass, its gray surface reflected like a mirror, and saplings and shrubs had been cleared within 100 yards of the ring.

"It's coated in a polyalloy rated to withstand several thousand degrees," the D1 robot said. "The ring extends down to bedrock to prevent tunneling efforts."

"It's quite the technical achievement," Grandma Betsy said.

"Cranes and trucks and thousands of robots," the D1 said. "Ore from southern mines fed blast furnaces."

"Who's it supposed to keep out?" Theodore asked.

Although he'd never seen the Great Wall of China in person, Theodore had looked at pictures and maps for a report at school, researching everything from the origins hundreds of years before the Qin dynasty to the ongoing efforts to expand the wall across several millennia and many thousands of miles.

"Before the ring," the D1 said. "The Luminary thwarted several plots to disrupt local utilities and the electrical grid. As a result, the entire city remains a high-security zone. Everyone lives under The Watchful Eye."

"The Watchful Eye?" Theodore asked.

"Optical collectors," the D1 said. "Peepstones connected to viewscreens."

"Cameras," Theodore said.

"Like the ones at your school," Grandma Betsy said.

Lanterns hovered midway up the wall, swaying with the breeze. Slushy mud had given way to crabgrass, greenery broken only by triangular bricks that pointed to an intercom beside a knobless metal door. So far as Theodore could see, looking left and looking right, there were no other doors or entrances or exits of any kind.

"Go ahead," the mannequin said. "Ring in."

"Go ahead," Grandma Betsy said.

Immediately as Theodore pressed the red square button to the left of the intercom's speaker, the sound of a throat being cleared crackled from the box.

"If you will wait a moment there," it said. "To protocol we must adhere."

"Boffins," Gary said.

The bigfoot adjusted his backpack straps, and the mannequin flicked the side of the intercom with its wooden finger, producing a muffled plunking sound. The robot looked up, and a small lantern floated over the top of the wall before dropping down for a closer look, light flickering from its lamp while a glass eyeball on a small arm extended from the underside.

"How cute," Grandma Betsy said.

She waved, and the intercom crackled a second time, with a different, deeper voice replacing the first speaker.

"Please state your business loud and clear," the voice said. "We've had no notice guests were near."

"My full name," Grandma Betsy said. "Is Betsy Judith Lyman, and I'm here with my grandson, Theodore and a few friends we've met along the way. We're seeking an audience with the Grand Luminary in the hopes that he can send us home."

The lantern with the glass eyeball drifted closer, listing sideways as it moved, its little arm twisting for a better view. When the speaker crackled a third time, a new voice, this time softer and smoother, spoke with warm tones.

"We'll need you to provide your town, prefecture, country, empire, galaxy, dimension, pocket universe, or subterranean nightmare realm of origin," the speaker said.

"Maybe we should go," Gary said.

"It'll be fine," Grandma Betsy said. "They're just asking for a little info. It's like going through customs at the airport."

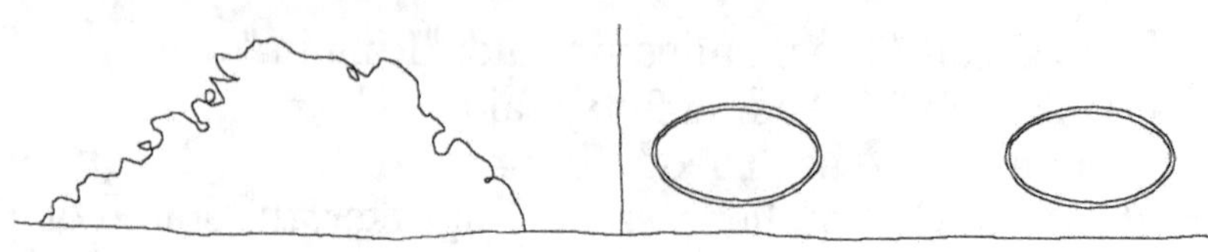

"We're from Earth," Theodore said.

"More precisely, Wisconsin," Grandma Betsy said.

After a cough, the third voice continued.

"Is anyone in your party in the possession of weapons, invasive species, corrosive chemicals, untested warp field technologies, superheated extradimensional vapors, radioactive materials, or other objects capable of widespread destruction?" the voice asked.

"I certainly hope not," Grandma Betsy said.

"Do we have your consent to be scanned?" the voice asked.

"Be my guest," Grandma Betsy said.

Bolts slid inside the metal door, and it swung open, revealing a wide hallway that led to blast shields. The robot went first, followed by the mannequin and Theodore, while Grandma Betsy followed Gary, who had to stoop to make it through the opening. A waist-high conveyor led into a dark hole in the wall, and a speaker on the ceiling chirped, then explained that everyone needed to place their personal belongings in the bins provided.

"Your items will be returned," the third voice said. "We want to avoid any chance of accidental incineration."

"We'll take Calipso with us, Theodore," Grandma Betsy said.

Gary set his crate on the belt, and the mannequin turned out its pockets to show it had nothing to deposit. The D1 robot stuck its finger into a small hole in the wall, and its eyes dimmed while Theodore unbuttoned his backpack, lifting out a sleepy Calipso before sending the bag down the conveyor.

"For newly-arrived earthlings seeking an audience with the Grand Luminary, printed maps will be provided in the lobby," the third voice said. "Please be reminded that over-sized cryptids must be registered with the Office of the Umpossible within 72 hours or risk expulsion from the city limits. Additionally, those traveling with animated objects and robots are encouraged to have their units serviced at one of Centrum City's many kiosks and vendor stalls."

"They have really specific announcements," Theodore said.

"That they do," Grandma Betsy said.

She set down her bag, and the door to the outside sealed itself as overhead lights blinked, tinting the room an amber color.

"Scan underway," a voice said. "Please refrain from sudden movements."

A copper tinge filled the air, followed by the smell of disinfectant.

"Everything's a process," Gary said.

"Much of life," Grandma Betsy said. "Is learning how to wait."

The D1 robot withdrew its finger from the wall, eyes brightening.

"The good news," it said. "Is that they're letting us through."

Indeed, as the D1 spoke, normal overhead lighting returned, and a hatch opened in the ceiling. A blue boffin hand dropped five temporary visitor passes on lanyard necklaces, passes that fell to the floor with pictures of the mannequin, the D1, Gary, Theodore, and Grandma Betsy, pictures that had been taken while they stood at the outside intercom. One smaller set of tags, fitted to a cat-sized collar, was clearly for Calipso.

"Centrum City is a melting pot," the mannequin said. "A place of industry and rare talent."

"Make sure not to stare at people," Grandma Betsy said. "Unless they stare at you. Then stare back even harder."

"And stick my tongue out?" Theodore asked.

"If you want to get it cut off," Gary said.

A motor engaged, and a section of the blast shields moved on a steel track. On the other side, a shiny robot waited beyond the conveyor belt with Gary's crate and Theodore's backpack and Grandma Betsy's cloth bag.

"A pair of boots in your possession," the robot said. "Formerly belonged to the governor of the Northland territories and has been flagged as an object of interest by the Grand Luminary."

"They were a gift," Grandma Betsy said.

She squeezed Theodore's hand, and the D1 unit fastened the collar around Calipso's neck before setting her in the backpack.

"As such," the shining robot said. "Your immediate presence is requested at the library."

The robot gestured to automatic doors beyond red leather couches at the back of the room, doors that opened to the neon lights of barges floating past cafes and bakeries and apothecary shops built into terraced hillsides punctuated by glass towers and hanging gardens, cobblestone streets filled with fruit carts and children chasing balls with sticks, a metropolis of stucco high-rises and crystal skyscrapers, a city that positively glowed.

Traveling to the Library

The streets of Centrum city curled around split-level villas and pyramid-shaped high-rises joined by paths bending and forking through small groves of trees, roads meandering to quartz spires and sunken gardens. Here and there, balconies hung over food vendor stalls and berry-laden bushes, whereas juice bars and roadside jewelers occupied the lower levels of shopping plazas. Grandma Betsy and Theodore took the lead through open-air markets, followed closely by the mannequin and the D1 robot and Gary, everyone marveling at the silver trams that ferried passengers between platform stations.

"It reminds me of Europe," Grandma Betsy said.

"It's like a videogame," Theodore said.

"It's certainly better than being bolted to a rack," the mannequin said.

"Do you know which way to go?" the D1 robot asked.

Packages and letters shot through pneumatic tubes that ran up walls and across busy intersections, canisters speeding through pipes like the ones Theodore had seen at the bank drive through.

"It would certainly help," Grandma Betsy said. "If there were street signs and building numbers."

"The robot at the gates said to walk straight ahead until we run into the Tree of Life, then look for a moss-covered bunker," Theodore said.

"Several miles due south of our current position," the D1 said. "At the edge of the park in the city center, steps lead down into the book stacks."

An elevated railway rose towards the downtown skyline, and the roads widened as the group passed wildflower rain gardens, bluebells nodding above creeping charlie and purslane, butterflies fluttering above beds of phlox and milkweed ringed by red brick retaining walls. Cloud cover had burned off, and greenhouse glass glinted in the late-afternoon sun, south-facing nurseries built into rolling swells while vining plants hung from botanical grow labs and vertical hydroponic farms installed up the sides of skyscrapers.

"Most of the food that feeds the locals is grown within the city walls," Gary said.

"That's quite an achievement," Grandma Betsy said.

She had already taken off her hat and gloves and winter jacket, as had Theodore, walking with his puffy coat tied around his waist. The shift from the snowy Northlands to the temperate warmth of Centrum City had been gradual enough that it felt natural, even routine, as though the transition to bright sunshine took place as a matter of course. Here and there, Boffins passed on bicycles and rang small bells as they approached intersections. Trogs, with their long legs and stubby forehead horns, wore coveralls and rode shaggy bighorn sheep the size of small cars. Occasionally, a ram passed pulling a carriage, and children waved from rear benches.

"It's a good spot to stop and watch the world go by," Grandma Betsy said.

"A place to see and be seen," the mannequin said.

The Tree of Life came into view as everyone passed through a public square, massive branches arching alongside skyspires and descending freighters attended to by airborne fleets of drones that guided and slowed the cargo ships as they arrived and departed from elevated platforms.

"Before the Luminary," the mannequin said. "Elven aristocrats maintained palatial estates."

"That changed, obviously," Theodore said.

"Tradition governed land use," the mannequin said. "One of the elven council members was friendly to the Luminary, and before long, factories and buildings were going up everywhere."

"It took them by surprise," Gary said.

"A man with a head for business," Grandma Betsy said. "Tell me about the elves."

"What about the elves?" the mannequin said.

"You've said they can turn people into gold, or invisible," Grandma Betsy said.

On a sloping green space at the base of a tower, a family of Zards sunned themselves on beach towels, swimsuits over yellow-gray scales soaking up the last rays before sunset. Whereas Trogs had small, distinctive antlers that protruded from their hairlines, Zard scale patterns appeared uniform and symmetrical, save for green-yellow variations and iridescent faces that shifted like the hologram baseball cards Theodore had gotten for his birthday.

"Elves are famously unpredictable," the mannequin said. "Some control the weather. Others read minds or pull fish from rivers with a snap of their fingers."

"Each develops differently," Gary said.

"How many elves have you met?" Theodore asked.

"Thankfully, none," the mannequin said.

Overhead, a barge drifted past, slowing, its steel hull glinting as Boffin sailors tossed mooring lines from the top deck.

"Elven delegations were the most demanding customers at Mr. Glum's lodges," the D1 said. "They'd complain about the speed of the resort's chair lifts and the time it took for water to get hot in the ski chalets. They'd criticize staff putting mint chocolates on bed pillows."

"Not to mention the invisible turkeys," Theodore said.

The sidewalk curved downhill, winding through obsidian towers that were joined, at the upper levels, by rope bridges and laundry lines. Their bodies reflected in black glass, Grandma Betsy and Theodore and the mannequin stepped onto a tree-bound tram, followed by Gary and the D1 robot. A Boffin conductor waved from a booth at the front of the railcar, which accelerated down a metal track the minute the doors hissed shut.

"I imagine," Grandma Betsy said. "That aristocrats are spoiled, no matter where they come from."

The tram hummed down the middle of the street, passing Zard fishmongers and Trog leather merchants, artisans working from shops nestled into giant twisting roots that jutted from the ground. Nearby, freight elevators ascended from the bases of gleaming skyspires, and cables held cargo ships to docks hundreds of feet in the air, structures dwarfed only by the Tree of Life with its upper limbs encircled by wispy clouds.

"If the Luminary's a human," Theodore said. "How come the elves didn't just throw him off the top of a mountain or poison him or something?"

"You're forgetting the importance of the Tree of Life to the ruling council," Gary said. "They never considered that he would hold them hostage to it."

"Elves tend to have a long-term view of things," the mannequin said. "Or so I've been told."

"A lot can happen in a century," the D1 said.

"The Luminary's been here 100 years?" Theodore asked.

Slowing for a platform, gears in the tram's undercarriage squealed and groaned. The Boffin conductor, a smiling gent with a white goatee, raised his gray cap and nodded to the opening doors.

"Please watch your step and take your things," he said. "This tram returns north to the Ring."

Theodore followed Gary out onto a tiled platform and down concrete steps to an archway that opened onto a street shaded by enormous branches with leaves the size of queen-sized beds.

"It seems," Grandma Betsy said. "A great many things are different here from what we're used to."

"I'll say," Theodore said. "The tree looks like a mountain."

Indeed, roots thicker than apartment buildings became sheets of bark hundreds of feet wide, and the trunk of the Tree of Life rose like the face of a sheer cliff, a wall broken only by boughs that spread out across the city center, a canopy that blocked out the sun and would have shrouded the ground in darkness, were it not for streetlights and floating lanterns and ropes of neon bulbs suspended from roof overhangs.

"It is a beautiful tree," Grandma Betsy said.

"It holds Um together," Gary said.

Thankfully, the stone steps of the public library were around the corner from the tram exit, granite stairs leading down to Um's quiet, subterranean stacks, collections staffed by Z7 droids wearing green woolen jackets over starched shirts and matching green trousers, robots shelving books with white cotton gloves while the Grand Luminary, having already eaten his morning oatmeal, sat beyond the repositories of his inner sanctum and stared at computer code.

The Grand Luminary

Only humans were allowed to enter the conference room, and its walls were mostly composed of one-way glass, allowing those inside to see out, while outsiders could not see in. In the waiting area, Theodore fed Calipso a slice of smoked salmon and left the catpack, as he'd come to call the backpack, with the mannequin, Gary, and the D1 unit, who promised to look after her during the meeting.

"Put in a good word for me," the mannequin said. "I'm hoping they'll let me get lost in the nonfiction section for a few decades."

"And if you could check," the D1 said. "I'd appreciate code updates to grant me the freedom to choose my own destiny."

"Remind him that the lands around the city have fallen into ruin, and treasures are being swallowed by the forest," Gary said.

Overhead fans blew cool air across overstuffed chairs and leather couches, and the conference door sealed as Grandma Betsy set her bag on a central table. An overhead projector flickered on, and the face of a clean-shaven man with slicked-back hair appeared on a white screen that descended from a ceiling gap.

"I," the face said. "Am the Grand Luminary."

He squinted, leaning in, pupils constricting.

"I've been informed," he said. "That you claim to be humans carrying the boots of a recently-deceased elven governor of the Northland realm. Please present yourselves, that I may verify your outlandish claims."

A small droid floated from an air vent and approached Theodore, bobbing gently, its twin camera lenses focusing.

"You don't look like you're 100," Theodore said.

"Excuse me?" the Luminary asked.

"We've been told you came here nearly a century ago,"

Grandma Betsy said. "You don't even have graying hair."

"Almost nobody in Wisconsin makes it 100 years," Theodore said. "But if they do, they're in wheelchairs and covered in wrinkles."

The overhead projector switched off, and for a moment, Theodore was certain he had done something wrong. The levitating droid drifted back, its lens apertures opening as it descended to a small charging station.

"Pomp and circumstance," Grandma Betsy said.

"What's that mean?" Theodore asked.

"It means, people like to dress up and make things seem important."

At the back of the room, a black section of glass slid sideways, and the Grand Luminary strolled into the room, followed by a Z7 robot that carried a plate of gingersnap cookies and wore a long leather jacket.

"Ebeneezer Ulysses Burroughs, formerly of Shawtown, Wisconsin," the Luminary said. "So happy to make your acquaintance."

The Luminary smiled and shook everyone's hands, motioning for the droid to set down the gingersnaps.

"We were driving in a snowstorm, and we ended up here," Theodore said.

"I'm Betsy Lyman, out of the La Crosse area," Grandma Betsy said. "And this is my well-intentioned grandson."

"Goodness, goodness, goodness," the Luminary said. "It's fortunate that you're from my neck of the woods and not Cairo or Singapore or the outskirts of Lima. Imagine how much trouble we'd have without a common language. In any case, do enjoy a cookie, and I hope you'll tell me about yourselves."

"Mr. Burroughs?" Theodore asked.

"Do call me Eb," the Luminary said.

Wearing a topcoat over a white dress shirt and a coal-colored vest with a matching tie, Eb ran a hand through his springy brown hair.

"Please," he said. "Go ahead."

"I've lived in a house on the bluffs for over 40 years," Grandma Betsy said. "During a blizzard, we slid off the road and somehow ended up north of here, where we ran over Governor Eyebright."

"Eyebright," Eb said. "Well, you certainly have my gratitude."

"Right," Grandma Betsy said. "In any case, we'd like to go home."

Theodore took a cookie from the tray, and a blend of cinnamon, ginger, and molasses dissolved in his mouth as he bit down.

"I believe I can assist you," Eb said. "Albeit with some difficulty on my part. What I'd like to propose is a small amount of assistance and an information exchange."

"Meaning what?" Grandma Betsy asked.

"Crossovers from Trogs and Boffins and Zards occur with a fair amount of regularity," Eb said. "Unfortunately, Earth is a somewhat tougher nut to crack. While my researchers have had considerable success reverse-engineering advancements from objects that find their way to Um, living things seldom make their way across."

Eb pulled a small cube from his pocket and set it on the table. As he touched a button on the side, a light shone from the top, and the holograms of four planets spun in the air.

"I have a strange question," Grandma Betsy said.

"I can only imagine," Eb said.

"Where," she asked. "Where exactly are we?"

The Z7 robot in the leather jacket flipped a switch on the wall, and the projector screen withdrew into the ceiling gap.

"Let's view Um as an overlap between at least four, likely five or six, dimensions," Eb said. "Every time someone isn't looking or a tree falls and nobody hears it, that's where Um is. Every time a dog barks at nothing, that's Um."

"How'd you get here?" Theodore asked.

Eb's smile wavered, and he waved off the Z7 unit.

"I'll keep the story short," he said. "I was traveling to a conference with my esteemed Professor Muffley when we met with a torrential downpour and high winds that drove us from the road, overturning our vehicle. I briefly lost consciousness, and when I awoke, I found myself in an enormous vegetable garden owned by a family of elves. Believing I must be suffering from head trauma, I sought out medical attention, only to find I was no longer on Earth. Due to a series of unconventional medical procedures, I'm here nearly a century later."

Eb plucked the cube from the table, and its hologram projection vanished as he handed it to Grandma Betsy.

"One thing that I request," he said. "Is that you bring this cube with you and press the red button when you reach Earth. Should you agree to be my test pilots, you'll be traveling in an experimental vehicle of my own design."

"And?" Grandma Betsy asked.

"And," Eb said. "The presence of humans remains very rare in Um, meaning that people greet you with a mix of wonder and awe."

Eb took a gingersnap and broke off an edge piece.

"This is no small request," he said. "But you'll need to remove Oja, a member of the elven council, if you want my help."

"How do you mean, remove?" Grandma Betsy asked.

"That," Eb said. "Is up to you. I will, however, provide transport."

He ate his cookie slowly, squinting as he nodded at Gary, the mannequin, and the D1 unit through the one-way glass.

"In my experience," Eb said. "Everyone wants something. I'm sure your companions have goals and aspirations, much as you do."

Theodore brushed crumbs onto the gingersnap tray.

"The mannequin," Theodore said. "Only wants to be allowed to read in the library."

"Naturally," Eb said.

"And the D1 hopes you can change its code," Theodore said.

"All within the realm of possibility," Eb said.

"Gary, the bigfoot," Grandma Betsy said. "Hopes to inspire people to return to their communities in the forests."

"People have swarmed to Centrum City for decades," Eb said.

Grandma Betsy held up the cube.

"And what will this thing do?" she asked.

Eb's smile returned, and he smoothed the sleeves of his overcoat.

"The cube," he said. "Will produce a signal across dimensions, much like a radio wave. By better calibrating my instruments, I hope to create a stable portal between Um and Earth."

Eb stood and walked to the doorway at the back of the room.

"Additionally, I'll need the boots you recovered from the body of Governor Eyebright, as they're imbued with ancient energies that are difficult to come by," he said. "Now, if you'll permit me to take you on a tour of the Sublime Industries Research and Development department, I'd be delighted."

Beneath the library, labs spread out like the runners of a potato plant. Long hallways descended and branched, leading to enclosures housing fabrication workshops and hermetically-sealed grow spaces filled with Boffin engineers who wore protective smocks and goggles. Between swinging doors, Theodore caught glimpses of droids pouring molten metal from crucibles into ceramic molds. Through clear plastic, he watched a robotic arm connect tiny wires to printed circuit boards while drones installed a hovercycle's impulse projectors and tuned the frame-mounted gyroscopes. Deeper in the facility, test bots sped around an elliptical track, motors whirring, steel frames streaking like bullets.

"The facility must've taken a long time to build," Grandma Betsy said. "It's quite extensive."

"The hardest part has been taking care not to accidentally damage the Tree of Life, as we're very close to its enormous root system," Eb said. "It took decades of diplomacy to be allowed to study it properly."

"If you're 100 years old," Theodore said. "Everyone you knew must be dead."

"Theodore," Grandma Betsy said.

Eb turned down a hallway lit by bright fluorescent lights and lifted a plastic wall flap, revealing a small hangar. Cables hung from open panels under a minivan-sized flying saucer, and lab techs, wearing anti-static coveralls, snapped ceramic capacitors into place.

"Boffins are naturally mechanically inclined, at least compared to humans," Eb said. "They've been instrumental in integrating Earth's artifacts into Um's rich technological tapestry."

"I suppose there's one of you and many thousands of them," Grandma Betsy said.

"Boffins number in the hundreds of thousands," Eb

said. "Once Centrum City became a sanctuary from the excesses of elven governors, I had an immediate base of workers designing factories. Automated innovation, we called it. Soon, machines were building machines. Propellantless thrusters transformed the importing of goods. Medical research made chronic conditions a thing of the past."

A Boffin worker scooted from beneath the saucer and flipped a switch on a board connected to a recessed instrument panel before stepping back to a safe distance. With a hum, the saucer rose, held in place by steel cords that were bolted to the walls.

"Over the last 10 years, we've been adding taller and taller buildings within the city," Eb said.

Across the room, a Z7 droid carried a microwave-sized cyclotron to the techs, who snapped rails on the sides before sliding it into an open utility hatch and ratcheting the unit into place.

"We don't have flying cars in Wisconsin," Theodore said. "Or robots anything like the ones around here. Or walking, talking mannequins."

"No?" Eb asked.

"We do have wireless everything," Theodore said. "And refrigerators."

"Wireless?" Eb asked.

"Telecommunications," Grandma Betsy said.

"Internet," Theodore said. "For laptops and cell phones. My mom has a Kindle."

Standing on his tiptoes, a worker switched off the saucer's propulsion system, and the disk grew quiet, drifting down to the rubber pads of a small landing platform.

"During my lifetime," Grandma Betsy said. "We went from slide rules to handheld computers."

The lab's Z7 droid held a pressurized tank in place, and a Boffin tech tightened a clamp.

"By all accounts," Eb said. "Um's industrial revolution predated advances on Earth but was more limited in scope. Even before my arrival, the Northlands had a dozen polytechnic schools, institutions fueled by Boffin tinkerers and a faction of elf enthusiasts."

"I suppose Boffin, Trog, and Zard civilizations all had their own technologies," Grandma Betsy said.

"As do all empires across time," Eb said.

After securing cables behind a pressure line, a drone drifted to the top of the saucer and opened a small panel, revealing a tiny ball of plasma contained between copper-wrapped toroids.

"By my calculation," Eb said. "Elves have over-relied on their inborn talents and failed to fully cultivate Um's potential."

"Which is?" Grandma Betsy asked.

"Comfort, joy, knowledge," Eb said. "We must grab the future and dance as we change it and it changes us."

The plasma ball at the top of the saucer grew, then flickered, then collapsed, and a small puff of smoke accompanied a sizzling sound. The Z7 drone clicked a button, and a bell sounded, momentarily, before a vacuum hose dropped from a ceiling port.

"I expect the vehicle should be operational within a matter of days," Eb said. "In the meantime, you'll be traveling to the council towers in Dammerung to act as my surrogates."

"Surrogates?" Theodore asked.

"He wants us to speak for him," Grandma Betsy said.

"Regarding Oja," Eb said.

As robots glued heat tiles to the saucer's outer shell, Grandma Betsy crossed her arms, frowning.

"We'll need the boots as collateral," she said.

"Excuse me?" Eb asked.

"You're asking us to take a lot on faith," she said. "And we've only just met."

Eb raised an eyebrow and pursed his lips. He squinted and drummed his fingers on his leg.

"I could have taken the boots by force the minute you were within earshot of the city," he said.

"But it sounds like it helps you, for whatever reason, if we talk to these council people," Grandma Betsy said. "Which I'm willing to do, because I'd like to get my grandson home safe and sound."

For a moment, the room was nearly silent. Fans hummed, and a Boffin tech tightened the nozzle on a pressurized tank. Near the saucer's rim, the Z7 bot closed the covering that housed the toroids. Grandma Betsy clutched her cloth grocery bag, and Theodore watched the vacuum hose retreat upwards.

"Then it's settled," Eb said.

"It's settled?" Theodore asked.

The Grand Luminary's smile returned, and he walked back the way they had come, lifting the doorway's plastic flap.

"I'll get you and your friends safely to Dammerung, such that you can enact Oja's departure from the council," Eb said. "Upon your return, I will gladly send you and the boots on your merry way."

"And you'll help Gary and the mannequin and the D1 unit," Theodore said.

"Yes, yes," Eb said. "All things in good time. Now, if we would be so good as to return to the conference room, my attendants should have cakes and coffee waiting."

Grandma Betsy followed the Luminary into the hallway, and as Theodore ducked under the flap, he felt momentary tension dissolve, the kind of shift he'd noticed when his dad found lost minivan keys between the seats and took everybody out for hot cocoa. For their part, the Boffin techs breathed easier as the humans left the room, blue skin lightening as they continued securing capacitors to the saucer's undercarriage.

"I'll inform Councilor Bell that I have a delegation on its way," Eb said. "Before you leave, we'll go over the dynamics of elven social graces. I wouldn't want to send you in blind."

"We are newly arrived, after all," Grandma Betsy said.

Eb turned down a long hallway, sidestepping wooden

crates and stacked insulation and a Z7 droid that carried several lengths of conduit.

"The main thing to remember," Eb said. "Is that they're going to say a lot of bad things about me. And some of those things are true."

"Oh?" Grandma Betsy said.

"I've worked with the council for decades, and we haven't always gotten along," Eb said. "But I certainly never intentionally crashed a barge through the main gates of their castle."

"Good to know," Grandma Betsy said.

"And I had no idea the barge was filled with stink beetles," Eb said.

"That's really specific," Theodore said.

The Luminary pressed a glowing button on the wall, and elevator doors hissed open.

"And I was entirely unprepared for Oja's proposal of marriage," Eb said.

"Now I'm just confused," Grandma Betsy said.

"As I am, my dear," Eb said. "As am I."

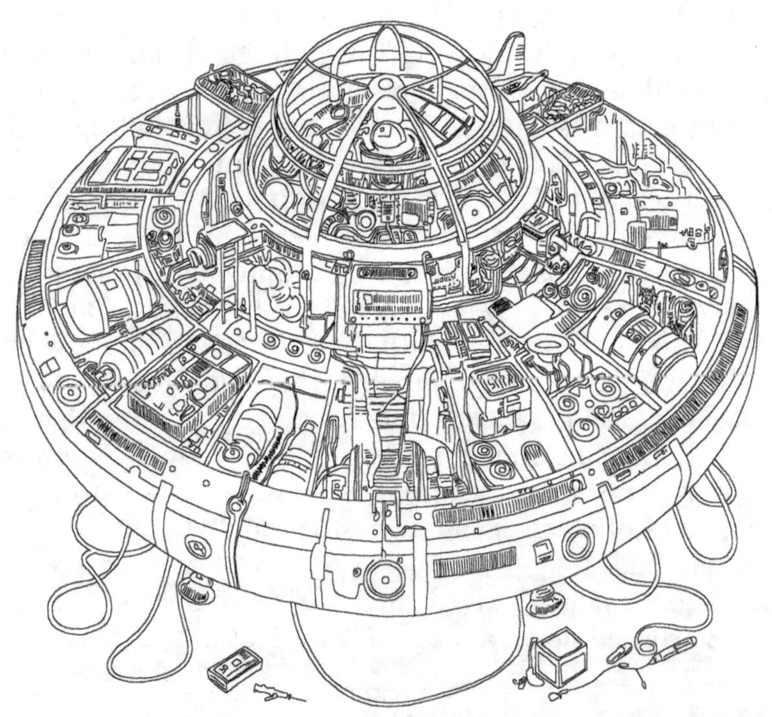

The Journey to Dammerung

At the top of the Grand Luminary's personal skyspire, an accordion-style skybridge extended and sealed around the doorway of a waiting airship. The mannequin was the first to enter, quickly seating itself in a booth with a bird's eye view of Centrum City. Skyscrapers gleamed in the setting sun. From above, pyramid high-rises looked like anthills, and freighters bobbed above tiny trees like plump bumblebees dusting themselves with pollen. Having already gained temporary patron access to the library and having checked out a pocket edition on the scientific opinions of Um's greatest scholars, the mannequin contented itself with the quiet turning of pages. The D1 robot carried a trunk filled with gifts for the elves, which the Grand Luminary had promised would not explode, as it walked past Gary, who took up two seats and sat with his furry head brushing the overhanging storage compartment.

"By eccentric," Grandma Betsy said. "I mean Eb is unconventional and strange. I never said he was a terrible person."

"It seems like you don't totally believe the things he says," Theodore said.

Grandma Betsy stowed her bag and plopped down opposite the mannequin, leaning against the padded back of the booth. Beyond comfortable window seats separated by swaying chandeliers, the airship's spacious interior included a soup station and a flat-topped grill beneath an over-sized oven hood. In the far front, crammed into the nose of the craft, a Boffin pilot waved before turning and flipping switches on an instrument panel.

"I simply wanted to note that Eb is outlandish," Grandma Betsy said.

Theodore held Calipso, one hand under her feet, the other under her front legs with his fingers scratching her neck. He slid in beside his grandmother, who had taken off her glasses and was rubbing her eyes.

"It's not his fault he's a goofball," Theodore said. "He's been here a long time with Boffins and Zards and Trogs and elves. Plus, he's building us a flying saucer."

"No argument there," Grandma Betsy said. "He's the one person with a plan to get us home."

A Z7 droid pulled the passenger door shut and twisted a giant lever, locking it in place as the cabin's lights dimmed.

"What do you think Zeb and the Boffins up north are doing with your car?" Theodore asked. "Do you think they got it fixed?"

"I can only imagine," Grandma Betsy said. "Would you mind it terribly, Theodore, if I rested my eyes?"

The airship floated free from its clamps on the skyspire dock, drifting sideways before it idled through wisps of low-level clouds and pushed ahead with steady thrust. Houses and tenements shrank, fading as the city and its outer ring grew dim, land quickly turning to the rusty reds and dull yellows of autumn, shady riverbanks meandering through sundown's sepia-toned rays, long shadows twisting across rocky foothills and deep lakes that reflected blobs of indigo and violet and scarlet at the edge of the sky.

"The western lands," Gary said. "Have a long, lingering twilight."

Theodore set Calipso down and retrieved a saucer from a small galley between the booths.

"What's the oddest creature you've ever seen in Um?" Theodore asked.

Gary stretched his legs, sweeping floor tiles with shaggy fur. At the front of the ship, the D1 bot tightened wall straps around the gift-filled trunk.

"In the Northlands," Gary said. "I've watched trolls play catch with boulders. I witnessed a leviathan swallow a cow whole. Two hundred years ago, I helped replant the talking bushes of Mu at the base of Mount Fels."

Gary leaned and scooped up Calipso, cradling the cat as she closed her eyes and rubbed her face against his thick, reddish-brown coat.

"But one thing you might find curious," Gary said. "Is that many years ago, my uncle had a cat. Yours is the second one I've ever seen."

"Cats aren't exactly rare in Wisconsin." Theodore said.

"We're as far from Wisconsin as you're ever likely to be, youngster," Gary said. "Let me take you back 150 years, and remember, my family's always been nomadic. Once, while crossing the rough highlands that separate the elves from the lands of the Boffins, my Uncle Aldo took an evening dip in a mountain stream. When he surfaced, he found himself near a human settlement outside a copper mine. Unfortunately, the prospectors did not prove friendly and Uncle Aldo hid in a barn, so the story goes, where he found a friendly kitten sleeping in the hay loft. A few days later, locals chased him off, and he again crossed the river to escape. He dove down to avoid gunfire, and when he reached the opposite banks, he had returned to Um. Somehow, the kitten had burrowed into his travel bag and come along for the ride."

Calipso kneaded Gary's belly with her front paws, claws retracting against his thick fur. Outside the airship's windows, dusk had fallen, cloaking the land in darkness, save for the lights of scattered buildings far below. To Theodore, it was as if the ground had become a mirror reflecting the night sky.

"Your uncle wasn't ever able to get back to Earth?" Theodore asked.

"Given the circumstances, I'm not sure why he would have wanted to," Gary said. "Until the Luminary arrived, humans were thought to be mythical creatures."

Grayish cloud puffs rolled past the windows, and the airship slowed as it banked to the right, gently decelerating as it descended from the night sky. Below, the spires of Dammerung grew from cliffs illuminated in pale green, giving the elven stronghold the appearance of twisted metal poles sticking up from a briar patch that had grown thick across an eroding hillside. Flying machines glowed like fireflies and whisked past as buildings on the ground grew larger. Brambles became long, branching apartment buildings connected by zip lines and trolleys and rope bridges. Smoke rose from open-air markets on flat-topped mushrooms. Gnarled branches housed penthouse suites with balconies overlooking knotholes at the ends of winding staircases. Lamps hung everywhere, and emerald brightness chased shadows across courtyards beneath bay windows surrounded by moss.

"We're almost there," the D1 unit said.

It nudged Grandma Betsy's shoulder, as she had nodded off, before tapping the mannequin's arm.

"The main station," the D1 said. "Is on the far side of the castle."

Elven drones dropped from above and escorted the airship down, their outer, semi-transparent shells glowing from within like giant light bulbs, and beyond the barbs and hedgerows of the main city, parapets topped stone walls that gave way to steeples and a bell tower.

"There used to be a larger diversity of life on Um, if my reading is to be trusted," the mannequin said.

"The same goes for Earth," Theodore said.

"During the second epoch, unicorn herds roamed the sunny steppes of the Eastlands, and clumps of ambrosia trees grew from the Muvian corridor to the ridges of the floating lake of Ken," the mannequin said.

"You have unicorns?" Theodore asked.

The airship circled the Dammerung, floating above the river canyon that ringed the city, gently dropping above dark waters to a landing zone circled by lights.

"Powdered unicorn horns turned into big business," Gary said.

"By the time the elven council appointed governors to oversee Um's regions, there were less than 1,000," the mannequin said.

Waving neon signaling lights, a Z7 droid walked backwards on the tarmac, and the airship swung low, nearly touching the ground before a team of bots secured mooring cables to anchor rings embedded in concrete blocks.

"There's a glowing man outside," Grandma Betsy said.

"He looks like a ghost," Theodore said.

This much was true. A single greeter wore long, gray robes and stood facing the airship's exit hatch. Pointed ear tips protruded from white hair, but the man's most eye-catching feature was a steady bioluminescent glow that radiated from the exposed skin on his head and hands.

"That's Councilor Bell, I believe," the D1 unit said.

"He's glowing," Theodore said.

"Yes," the D1 said. "All elves glow."

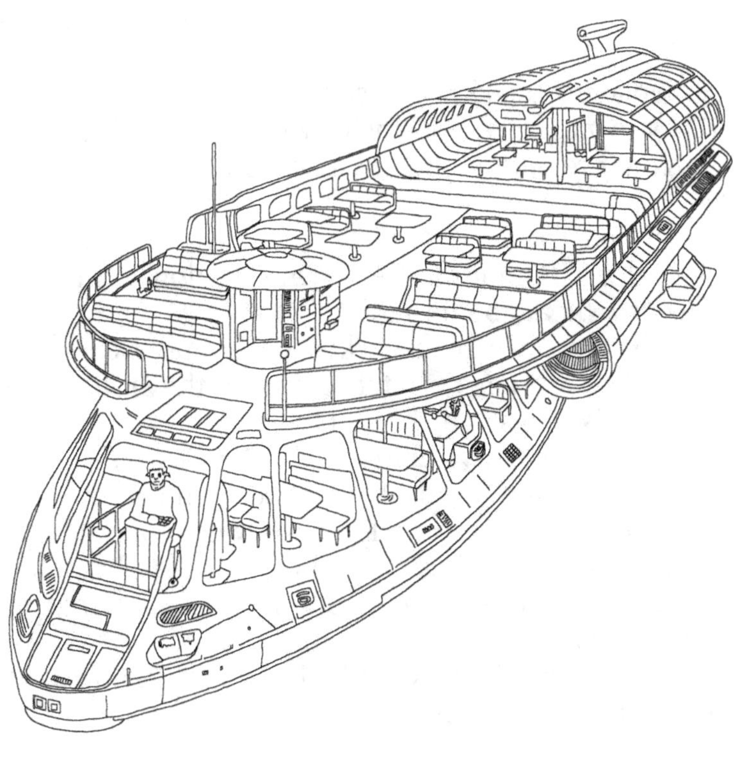

Meeting the Elves

Hovering globes lit the castle's inner chambers, and Councilor Bell spoke with a hollowness in his voice, a timbre that reminded Theodore of wind in a cave. The main hall, ringed by tall bookshelves, sank into the ground like an amphitheater, with stadium seating sloping to a huge circular table. Attendants, Boffins and Trogs, mostly, brought sweet cakes on silver trays, and soft sounds, even whispers and footfalls, projected throughout the room without any need for electrical amplification.

"My encounters with those of human birth are in truth quite limited," Bell said.

"We're quite new to the concept of elves," Grandma Betsy said.

"Except in movies," Theodore said. "And roleplaying books."

"Roleplaying books?" Bell asked.

"They're games you play with your friends," Theodore said. "You pretend to be a character. I was an elven mage."

"Oh?" Bell asked.

"Theodore," Grandma Betsy said. "I don't think our host needs to hear about that."

Bell leaned on a high-backed chair and cleared his throat. A falcon image stretched across the front of his robes, and his shoes had pointed toes.

"What do you do as a councilor?" Theodore asked.

A Trog servant, her horns wrapped in tinsel, set down a tray of cups and a porcelain teapot with steam wisping from the spout. Theodore was about to ask when she'd started growing horns, but it occurred to him that his grandmother would likely pinch his arm.

"As a steward, I work both day and night to undo problems in Um," Bell said.

Overhead, a globe flickered.

Fireflies floated like dust in the air.

Councilor Bell's yellow eyes peered from deep sockets, and bluish muscles moved beneath nearly-translucent skin, such that Theodore had a hard time reading the elf's expressions.

"Your grandson, if I tell the truth, reminds me of young Eb in Um," Bell said. "He had lots of zeal, and it seemed surreal. He had questions, and then some. If your boy's the same, then he's not to blame. But I hope you'll caution him. For the human Eb has defied our laws, and our patience grows quite thin."

Inside the cloak's hood, Bell's hair swayed like cobwebs, white strands framing gleaming skin. His eyes watched the mannequin stroll along bookcase-lined walls while the D1 robot set the trunk from the Luminary on the room's central table. Bell watched Gary yawn, revealing rows of canines in a cavernous jaw. He watched Grandma Betsy, who had seated herself in a heavy oak chair that had wraparound arms and a crushed velvet cushion with a matching backrest.

Fireflies floated, blinking on and off.

Theodore poured tea for his grandmother and the councilor, and the steam smelled of apple blossoms, which reminded the boy of Grandpa Frank's funeral at a small cemetery off a county road near an orchard. Trees with pink petals, he remembered. Little American flags rippled with the wind. Grandma Betsy had looked older when she smiled.

"We must ask that Eb ceases drawing sap from the base of the Tree of Life," Bell said. "There are deals he's made. He has debts unpaid, and he's always causing strife."

"If I may," Grandma Betsy said.

"Please," Bell said.

"Tell me what laws he's broken."

"Other than being a weirdo," Theodore said.

"Theodore Maxwell Lyman," Grandma Betsy said.

"He's a weirdo. He lives in a library with robots," Theodore said. "He has an army of drones."

The glow from Councilor Bell's eyes softened, and he smiled, producing a scroll from his robe's sleeve.

"In the first, Eb pollutes sacred lands, and he disobeys decrees. He has yet to pay back several loans from elven treasuries. There's been damage done to the properties of investors near and far. His indifference, to a great degree, brings us to the edge of war."

On the far side of the room, heavy oak doors swung open, and a tall elven woman strode into the hall, followed by a chorus of robed servants. Wearing riding breeches and a tunic with a falcon embroidered on the chest, the woman marched past the mannequin and the bookshelves on the far wall, making a beeline for Bell and Grandma Betsy.

"I was to be informed when they arrived," she said.

Tied by leather bands, thick, sea-foam-green braids spilled down her back, and she towered over Bell and Grandma Betsy, a hand on her sword hilt, emerald eyes flashing.

"I present to you, from the western lands in the Duchy of Mu, Oja," Bell said.

He raised his hand with a flourish, then turned to Grandma Betsy, who was blowing on her tea.

"Our diplomacy, in recent times, leaves something to be desired," he said.

"When I think about it, I suspect that the word we've been looking for, regarding Eb," Grandma Betsy said. "Is eccentric."

"He's a weirdo," Theodore reiterated.

Oja's eyes darkened to indigo, and violet veins streaked the amber glow of her cheeks. Gary, who had already gobbled down several trays of honey-sweetened biscuits, removed a flower arrangement from a nearby pedestal and drank water from a porcelain vase. The D1 robot, spotting crumbs on the table, removed a brush and a dustpan from its chest compartment and busied itself by sweeping up. Across the room, the mannequin, who had been engrossed in its book, raised a finger.

"Perhaps outlandish is the word you're looking for," the mannequin said.

"I say eccentric," Grandma Betsy said. "Because Eb is intelligent and unconventional, although I could say the same about many people we've met in Um. If it's true that he led the construction of Centrum City, then that is quite an achievement, in its own right."

"Also, he doesn't look 100 years old," Theodore said. "He isn't bald, and he doesn't even have gray hair."

"I'd like to interject," Oja said.

"Of course," Grandma Betsy said.

Oja plucked a linen napkin from a pile on the table and dabbed the corners of her mouth.

"By what means," Oja asked. "Have you traveled to Um?"

One of her attendants, a Boffin woman, stepped forward with a small box, setting it in Oja's hands.

"We shall measure any claims you make with an orb of certitude," she said. "But remember, lies will banish you to the floating lake of Ken."

"We shall do no such thing," Bell said.

Oja opened the box, and a blue fog spilled from a sphere the size of a baseball.

"Place your hand on the orb," she said. "Older woman, you will go first."

Grandma Betsy looked at Councilor Bell with a knitted brow, and he frowned with a subtle shake of his head, his white hair swaying like prairie grass. Theodore had seen chess players stare at pieces in a similar way, wheels turning in minds calculating moves on a board.

"Give me your hand," Oja said.

"You forget your place," Bell said.

"Perhaps unorthodox is the word you're looking for," the mannequin said.

Oja stepped towards Grandma Betsy, and Councilor Bell sighed.

"There's no need for this," he said.

He pursed his lips, and electrical arcs streamed from his nose and mouth to his pointer finger before jumping a second time to Oja's forehead, and for a moment, everything stopped. The D1 unit stood emptying the dustpan into a bucket. The mannequin reclined, book in hand, elbows to the bench. Gary had frosting on his furry fingers. Grandma Betsy gripped the arms of her chair like a plane was crashing, and Theodore watched Bell wink, ever so slowly.

"Don't mind us," Bell said. "It's just a little squabble."

Oja's eyes dimmed, and her lids fluttered; her shoulders slumped, and her face relaxed as she levitated, feet rising off the floor before she flew backwards, knocking servants to the hardwood as she sailed, head over heels, out through the doorway on the far side of the chambers.

Moth and the Reflecting Pool

The long hallways of the castle led to sealed research wings and smoky alchemy labs and verdant arboretums sustained by babbling fountains and hunks of granite that radiated ultraviolet light. Everywhere throughout the stronghold, manicured ivy and moss obscured the stone walls, with vines creeping along doorway arches and the beams that stretched across vaulted ceilings. Younger elves, Bell told the group, took on upkeep and maintenance roles, and indeed, curious heads peeked from smoky hearths and jar-filled storage rooms and cool larders stocked with salted meats as Grandma Betsy, Theodore, Gary, the mannequin, and the D1 robot followed the councilor's robes up winding staircases to a small bridge connecting the keep to the courtyard of the inner dormitories.

"The governors should arrive by nine," Bell said. "Until that time, you may wander these halls as you like."

"And Councilor Oja?" Grandma Betsy asked.

"You've no cause for concern," Bell said.

Beyond the base of the bridge, a circular entryway led to an atrium garden built around a reflecting pool, and placid surface tension mirrored the wide staircases, arching joists, and alcove statues that surrounded the tranquil shallows. In the still, glossy liquidity, Theodore watched translucent projections come in and out of focus; mages sprayed streams of fire at advancing ice giants. A massive tree battered castle gates with knobby branches.

"How do you make the movies play in the pool?" he asked.

"What do you see?" Bell asked.

"Wizards and magical creatures," Theodore said. "On a battlefield."

"Wizards?" Grandma Betsy asked.

"I," Gary said. "See the sylvan towers of Elysium

before fiery volcanic ash turned my homeland to ruin."

"It's hard to make out," the mannequin said. "But I'm watching lumberjacks fell trees in a forest."

"And I," the D1 robot said. "I see Zard work crews filling mining carts in the Eternal Desert."

"The aquifer that feeds the pool runs through the roots of the Tree of Life," Bell said. "Before the castle came to be, a pond showed visions of what was to come, of quarries carved in the foothills of mountains while Dammerung lit up the night. To the elders, it was the sign they were looking for."

"Is the pool alive?" Grandma Betsy asked. "Does it think the way we do?"

"I believe," Bell said. "It reflects thoughts the way a mirror reflects the light."

He led everyone up a flight of granite steps and along a balcony that branched into dormitory apartments furnished with pillow-covered mattresses and wardrobes and wooden desks fitted with inkwells and quill pens.

"The reflecting pool does not often repeat itself," Bell said. "It plays memories of the future and the past, no rhyme, no reason."

Bell clapped his hands, directing attendants as he walked, and after introducing Theodore and Grandma Betsy to an elderly elven servant named Moth, he bowed and left the group in bedchambers deep within the castle, encouraging everyone to rest after their journey. Of course, the mannequin had no personal experience of what sleep was, and the D1 unit had been designed for constant use, but Gary lounged across a padded sofa, and Grandma Betsy sat on the edge of a four-poster bed to untie her shoes, wiggling toes as she pulled a foot free.

"I wouldn't want to get on Bell's bad side," Theodore said.

"Or Oja's," Grandma Betsy said. "Or any of the elves, honestly."

"Both are formidable warriors," Gary said. "Or at least they were, at the battle of Greysung."

"The last great conflict before the creation of the elven council," the mannequin said.

"A conflict," the D1 robot said. "Which resulted in the governorships that exist to this very day."

"It was a squabble between high lords," Moth said, leaning in. "And I should know, because I was there. I'll have your beds done up in a moment's time."

A box of blooming moonflowers on the windowsill filled the room with sweetness, and in the outside courtyard, bats dove through swarms of bugs that hovered around the light poles, gorging themselves on fluttering insects.

Theodore set his water jug on a granite countertop and took in the room: textured comb patterns reached across the ceiling, touched only by the creepers that clung to stone walls and brass candle sconces. Besides the furniture, which reminded him of the rounded, lacquered edges of dressers at antique furniture shows he'd gone to with his mother, he noticed an intentionality to the placement of objects; everything was exactly where it needed to be. The mirror above the sink curved with the wall and gave a full view of the room. A back scratcher hung from the largest bed's headboard, and rows of colored inks lined the top shelf of a rolltop desk beside a painter's easel.

"In any case, it was a long time ago and the kind of thing best forgotten about," Moth said.

Despite a body bent by age, she glided across the room with ease, turning down sheets and comforters with the strong, thin hands that come from a lifetime of work. Soft, white hair flowed halfway down her back, and her robes, while brown and undecorated, rippled like silk as she busied herself setting out bath towels and filling a tray with cups and saucers.

"If you need me during your stay, there's a bell on a rope above each nightstand," she said.

"What was the battle about?" Theodore asked.

"The battle?" Moth asked.

"Greysung," Theodore said. "Where I'm from, we've had lots of wars."

He pressed the waist strap's release, then slid off his backpack, setting it on the floor. Calipso, who had been mewing softly within, poked a paw from under the top flap as Theodore undid the buttons and gently dumped her onto a footstool.

"As I recollect, it was difficult for some to accept that they might be stuck in Um," Moth said. "There were those who claimed Um was ours to take, but several elders disagreed. With no edicts from the empire, the House of the Falcon gained control."

The elderly elf bent to pet Calipso, who hopped to the ground and peeked around an armchair. Exploring her new environment, the cat sniffed at Gary's giant, hairy foot before circling the legs of the mannequin, who nearly fell to avoid stepping on her and was caught, in turn, by the D1 robot, who had busied itself laying blankets at the foot of Grandma Betsy's bed.

"In the end, Greysung burned," Moth said. "It's the sneaky side that most often wins wars."

"And everyone's still here in Um?" Theodore asked.

"We're stuck with each other," Moth said. "A colony cut off from its elders."

She pinched the air, and the room's glowing orbs, which floated near the ceiling, dimmed, humming like the white noise machine Theodore's parents ran at night, a continuous calm of soothing, looping waves like a record playing static over ocean tides. For days, the rush of events had kept Theodore from fully considering the possibility that he and his grandmother might be away from Earth indefinitely, and he felt a great tiredness as Moth set a kettle on glowing pads that quickly brought water to a boil; indeed, the trip to Centrum City and the voyage to Dammerung via the airship had made a return to Wisconsin feel just out of reach, but in the creaks and murmurs of the castle, with shadows draped across the furniture, Theodore felt Wisconsin spinning farther and

farther away. He imagined his fifth grade desk empty, footprints filling with snow on the backside of the sledding hill, the light on his front porch shrinking, flickering, twinkling as it grew more and more remote.

"If we're here for a while," Theodore said. "We should at least have some say in how things go."

Grandma Betsy, who had set her shoes on the room's accordion radiator, blinked and folded her hands on her knee.

"I agree," she said. "Wholeheartedly."

Dust floated on autumn light cast from thick windowpanes, and Grandma Betsy let herself fall back onto the bed's comforter.

"Our transportation should be ready by the time we get back to Centrum City," she said.

She left her glasses on a pillow and rubbed the dark circles under her eyes; she looked older, Theodore thought, wondering if he, too, looked drawn and pale. In the mirror, his eyes looked puffy, he thought, and he was only roused from his introspective moment by Moth setting cups of tea on end table coasters, wooden infuser balls floating in the steaming liquid.

"You have two friends in Oja and Bell," Moth said. "Oja seeks, in her own way, to save Eb from the governors' treachery."

At this, Gary sat up, and his couch creaked while the D1 robot slid a hot water bottle under the blankets at Grandma Betsy's feet. Across the room, the mannequin followed Theodore's lead and petted Calipso on the head, everyone unaware of the fact that Oja had been quietly aiding the Grand Luminary for many years, unaware that she had proposed marriage as a way to grant Eb rights in the eyes of the council, rights that could well save The Tree of Life, and by way of the thick, knobby roots that spread through every quadrant of Um, save the world.

An Illuminating Meeting

A ring of elves looked up from the amphitheater's circular table as Grandma Betsy and Theodore entered the council chambers. Governor Goldfinch wore a buckskin tunic with golden trim and silver accents while Governor Cloverfield's wings lay folded around the edges of her cloak. Councilor Bell sat between Oja and Governor Mourningdove, who wore matching rubies set into a padded leather blindfold, stones that shone with a bright, ruddy light that made it difficult to look at her directly. One seat remained empty on the far end, presumably reserved for the absent Governor Eyebright, and the council fell silent as the humans descended the steps to the high-backed chairs that faced the panel.

"When we were told a contingent had come from Earth," Governor Cloverfield said. "We were understandably skeptical."

"And yet, here you are," Governor Goldfinch said.

"Emissaries," Governor Mourningdove said. "Of the crafty variety."

"They've only recently arrived," Bell said.

"Eb's surrogates," Oja said.

Councilor Bell opened a drawer in the table's underside and removed a scroll, squinting as he unfurled the parchment.

"Accompanying the humans," he said. "Was a trunk of jewels and perfumes and a pair of ancient manticore horns as a gift."

"They seek to buy us off," Governor Cloverfield said.

"With trinkets and baubles," Governor Mourningdove said.

Grandma Betsy's chair scraped across the floor as she pulled it to the table and sat down.

"If I may," she said.

"By all means," Bell said.

"Do you have any experience in affairs of state?" Governor Goldfinch asked. "Any at all?"

Glasses at the end of her nose, Grandma Betsy leveled a stare at council, squinting as she breathed and leaned forward.

"When my son was young," Grandma Betsy said. "I was the head of the PTA."

She crossed her arms and shrugged.

"I've been involved with the League of Women Voters since Jimmy Carter was president," she said.

Her voice faltered, and she coughed, clearing her throat as punctuation.

"When Frank was still alive, we co-led presentations on the power of kindness at the Unitarian Fellowship," she said.

"Frank?" Bell asked.

"My husband," Grandma Betsy said. "He's passed."

"Where we're from," Theodore said. "She's a pretty big deal."

Across the table, Governor Cloverfield sat stone-faced as Governor Goldfinch leaned back, hands on his belly, tenting his fingers. Boffin attendants, serving from the left, set down plates of fruit, and Governor Mourningdove speared a piece of honeydew melon.

"It's usually best to keep things short and sweet," Grandma Betsy said. "Eb, the Grand Luminary, has confided in me that he will cease collecting sap from the Tree of Life if the council removes Oja from its ranks."

After pausing to cough into her jacket sleeve, Grandma Betsy wiped her mouth and licked her lips.

"Eb has also agreed to abandon his interests in elven affairs of state and seeks to develop Centrum City as an independent territory," she said.

"Outrageous," Governor Cloverfield said.

"Distractions," Governor Mourningdove said.

"I believe you've misunderstood the purpose of these proceedings," Governor Goldfinch said.

"Do tell," Grandma Betsy said.

A smile flickered across Governor Goldfinch's lips, and Theodore bit into a green apple, lips puckering at the sourness. Bell exchanged a glance with Oja, whose irises smoldered like glowing campfire coals, and she clenched her jaw.

"Since its inception, Centrum City has been an eyesore, a scab concealing the slow spread of gangrene," Goldfinch said. "A sickness permitted by fears that the cure would be worse than the disease."

His hands glowed as his voice grew louder; a yellow patch spread from his fingers, bubbling across the table.

"Each and every day," he said. "Drones spread your language to the farthest reaches of Um, filling children's heads with human ideas of progress and business and greed."

The tabletop hissed as the yellow blotch expanded, heat rolling from liquid gold that absorbed lacquered wood. Governor Goldfinch paused, lifting his hands, and the yellow spread stopped immediately, cooling in an instant.

"For these reasons, made especially urgent by the untimely death of Governor Eyebright, the voting governors have agreed to strike to the heart of the matter," he said.

"Every passing month puts us in a weaker and weaker position," Governor Cloverfield said.

"We risk having our subjects be entirely consumed by the ideas of Eb and his acolytes," Governor Mourningdove said.

Governor Goldfinch plucked a grape from a sagging bunch and popped it into his mouth.

"We've assembled a team of operatives who will neutralize Eb and disarm his threat to the Tree of Life," he said. "Additionally, pending investigation, all humans in Dammerung shall be confined to their quarters."

"It's been more than a century," Governor Mourningdove said.

"It has become a plague," Governor Cloverfield said.

Grandma Betsy snapped her fingers as Theodore took a big second bite of his apple. He felt slightly woozy, and bright spots floated across his field of vision.

"Am I to understand that we're prisoners?" Grandma Betsy asked.

"None of this has come to a vote," Bell said.

Governor Cloverfield skewered a cantaloupe slice with a salad fork. Governor Mourningdove poured herself tea from a glass kettle. Theodore swallowed, focusing on Councilor Bell, and the spots in his eyes floated to the periphery.

"Since human visitors to Um are rare," Grandma Betsy said. "Let me tell you about Earth."

At this, the elves, including Governor Goldfinch, took interest, scratching their chins as they blinked and leaned forward.

"I was born," Grandma Betsy said. "At a time when everyone believed terrible weapons might end the world, and Earth's superpowers have been stuck at a stalemate ever since. Millions, if not billions of people, suffer as a result."

She reached down and grasped Theodore's fingers, rubbing them between her palms.

"My grandson and I have been fortunate to live in the Midwest," she said. "We read books and go window shopping. In the mornings, I drink coffee and listen to wind chimes."

Oja's eyes softened; ruddy embers became flickering flames.

"I'll confess," Grandma Betsy said. "I don't know Eb's motives, but I can say I lived through the Bay of Pigs and the Cuban Missile Crisis."

"The Bay of Pigs?" Theodore asked.

"Long story short, I don't know why anyone would flirt with war," Grandma Betsy said.

She let go of Theodore's hand and put her palms together, fingers extended, as if in prayer.

"A relationship," she said. "Can always be repaired."

Governor Mourningdove sipped tea as Councilor Bell nodded and furled his scroll.

"Unfortunately, the decisions of the Governors are not up for debate, democratic or otherwise," Governor Goldfinch said.

"We came to a consensus the moment we arrived," Governor Cloverfield said.

"Operatives were dispatched several hours ago," Governor Mourningdove said.

"They should already be breaching the Ring's defenses," Governor Cloverfield said. "And they'll either succeed in deactivating Eb's machinations, or the fabric of Um will come apart following Eb's death."

Governor Goldfinch ate a second grape, and Theodore felt the wooziness return, a rush like the sensation of falling asleep. His legs sagged, and it was then that he fainted.

A Return to Centrum City

Theodore awoke surrounded by Grandma Betsy, the mannequin, the D1 unit, Gary, and Oja, who held a small radio with a crystal sticking out the side. Clouds clipped past the airship's windows, and as Theodore sat up, blankets slid off the bench that had served as his makeshift bed.

"Are we confined to quarters?" he asked.

"There's been a change in plans," Grandma Betsy said.

"I hope you don't mind a tag-along," Oja said.

She winked, and for the first time since meeting her, Theodore saw Oja smile, a wide grin revealing straight, sharp teeth that gleamed.

"She carried you through the castle like a sack of potatoes," Grandma Betsy said.

"Honestly, I thought Eb had clued you in," Oja said.

"Clued us in?" Theodore asked.

"Don't worry," the mannequin said. "You weren't the only ones in the dark."

As it leaned close, the soft tones of the mannequin's voice remained crisp and clear as they projected from the curves of a wooden head.

"We had no idea what was going on until Moth escorted us to the tarmac," it said. "We left in quite a hurry, I might add."

Arms extending, the D1 robot handed Theodore his backpack, which wiggled as Calipso pushed out her head.

"In the mad rush, the furry carnivore was nearly abandoned," the D1 said. "She hid beneath a wardrobe."

"We had to lure her with food," the mannequin said.

"She is a cat, after all," Gary said.

Oja switched on her handheld radio, and static crackled, tones rising and falling as she twisted a tuning knob; the hiss evened out, and a man's voice emerged, distorted but intelligible.

"Citizens are advised to seek shelter, as attacks are ongoing. Please remain indoors and await further instructions," the voice said. "Emergency droids have been dispatched to impacted areas and will assist rescue efforts."

"Bell was caught as off guard as I was," Oja said. "Everyone's played it close to the chest."

"It's incredibly reckless," Gary said.

"It's what Eb expected," Oja said.

She switched off her device, nodding towards the front of the ship and its view of forests that gave way to Centrum City's massive Ring and shimmering skyspires separated by the white dots of windows in pyramid high-rises. In the air above the city, energy bursts flickered as elven drones, tapered like light bulbs, streaked around crystal towers and skyscrapers, firing on floating barges and transmitter arrays. Triangular air defense ships launched from vents in the sides of armored silos, and smoke billowed from gaping holes in factories compromised by explosives and plasma discharges.

"I'll give you the short version," Oja said.

"No time like the present," Grandma Betsy said.

"It looks like the Fourth of July," Theodore said.

Pockets of ionized gas flashed as disabled vehicles limped to safety, thrusters firing to prevent drones and gyrocopters from colliding with the reinforced steel and obsidian glass of Centrum City's superstructures.

"Eb arrived in Um at a time of elven dominance. Greysung had fallen, and Um's regions had already been unified," Oja said.

Calipso hopped into Grandma Betsy's lap as the elderly woman leaned towards the window for a better look. On the ground below, mobile units had set up anti-aircraft ion cannons that fired charged bolts at low-flying elven drones.

"For a good, long while, the Council treated Eb like a celebrity," Oja said. "He took an interest in elven technology and thought to combine it with gadgets from

Earth. Governor Cloverfield granted him land and let him build Centrum City around the Tree of Life as an experiment. For decades, he was their curiosity, a pet project to check up on, an inventor whipping up new and fantastic doodads."

"A trendsetter," the mannequin said.

"A visionary," the D1 unit said.

"A catalyst," Gary said.

The airship slowed as it neared the Luminary's skyspire, and the explosions below were a bit louder, now. Chem trails from downed vehicles rose as colorful streaks stirred by the wind, and the wail of a siren rolled across the city.

"One thing I haven't mentioned," Oja said. "Is that humans rarely find their way to Um, but stray devices and appliances regularly show up in the Northlands. A lost toy here, a new piece of hardware there."

"I found a metal telescope after a hail storm, once," Gary said. "My cousin found a refrigerator in a gully."

"So Eb's been collecting everything he can find," Theodore said.

"From afar, he's been listening in on Earth's broadcasts for decades," Oja said.

"Keeping up with the news," Grandma Betsy said.

The accordion skybridge extended, and metal clamps gripped the side of the airship.

"At some point, the relationship between Eb and the governors soured," Grandma Betsy said.

Theodore put on his backpack while Grandma Betsy rubbed Calipso under the chin.

"Since your arrival," Oja said. "They've been worried you're the start of some kind of invasion."

The D1 unit picked the blankets up off the floor and folded them over its arm, and the mannequin sat with its head in its hands, listening alongside Gary, who appeared to have quickly nodded off.

"Elven aristocrats, as a general rule, don't have a good sense of humor," the mannequin said.

"But they're also not stupid," Oja said. "The governors only became critical of Eb when they realized they were losing Boffin and Trog and Zard workers to Centrum City. In large numbers, no less."

A nearby explosion set shivers through the skyspire as the airship's Boffin captain spun the cabin door's locking wheel and opened the exit.

"Do watch your step, look out below," the captain said. "Crashed ships are causing fires to grow."

Again the skyspire shook, and everyone rushed for the skybridge, nearly trampling a Z7 drone that accompanied a wide-eyed Boffin tech who wore a vest fitted with pliers and wrenches and bottles of oily fluids; the D1 robot stuffed Calipso into Theodore's backpack as they ran to a waiting lift, and the mannequin, excited by the loud city filled with explosions, jogged alongside Grandma Betsy, who limped, having gotten a charley horse from standing up too fast. Gary swayed and lumbered down the walkway, followed by Oja, who strolled with a hand on her sword hilt and did not appear concerned in the slightest.

"The most difficult part these last few days," Oja said. "Has been keeping up appearances. Everyone's been on pins and needles in anticipation of the governors."

"When we arrived at the castle, it seemed like Bell was less than pleased with you," the D1 unit said.

"And you with him," the mannequin said.

At this, Oja tapped her temple with her index finger.

"In Dammerung, the walls have eyes," she said. "Everyone has a role to play, and Bell plays his well."

She pressed a button, and the lift descended on a pillow of air along its hoistway, dropping through the spire's sprawling lobbies and lounges and retail outlets. On the sunny side of the building, several windows had been blown in, and droids were already vacuuming glass from food court tables.

"The bladed rings have already started cutting," Gary said.

The lift settled on an elevated platform in the spire's main hall, and glass doors hissed open. Theodore held his hands over his ears, for above the booming impacts of plasma cannons tearing holes in assembly plants and textile mills, a steady, low-pitched whine rose above smoke and sparks and conversation. Visible beyond pyramid high-rises and crystal monoliths, a huge crane with rotating blades sliced through the boughs of the Tree of Life, sending chunks of the canopy crashing to the ground, and plumes of what Theodore would eventually learn was sawdust filled the air, kicked up by the wind and falling as what appeared to be snow.

"I don't think Eb's bluffing," Grandma Betsy said.

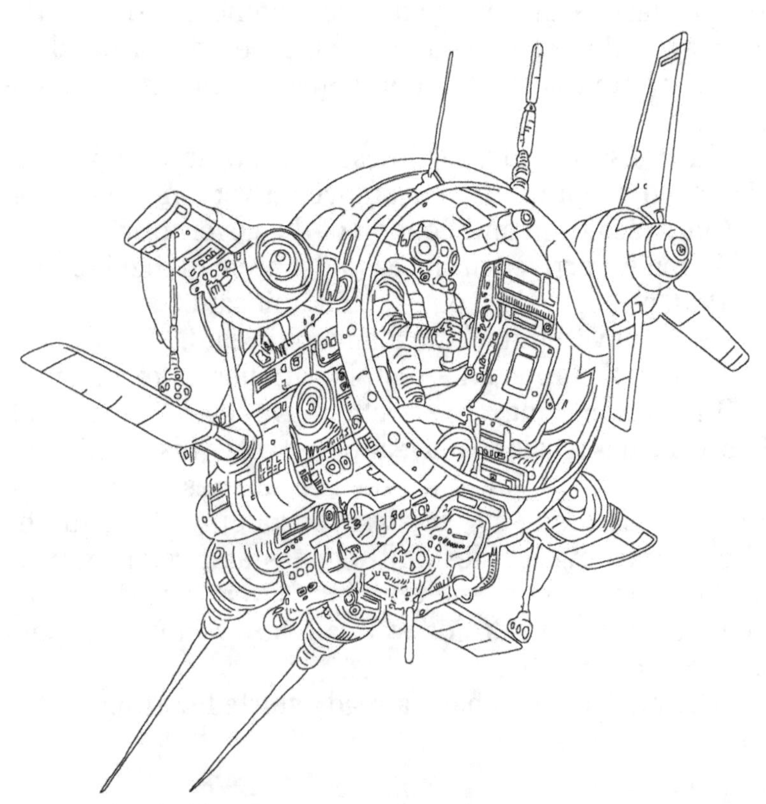

Eb Makes Good on his Word

The Z7 units stationed outside the Centrum City's library recognized Theodore and Grandma Betsy immediately and were under orders to bring everyone to the Luminary in the main conference room. Scanner droids floated through the bookshelves and the media stacks, sweeping the facility for would-be assassins or explosives or saboteurs, and Eb's attending Z7 unit, the one wearing the long leather jacket, pushed a cart topped with teapots and bottles of juices and rows of porcelain cups; on the underside, trays of cyclops cookies cooled above blueberry scones, and in a small storage compartment, savory biscuits waited to be plated with buttery pats.

"We brought your messages to the Council," Grandma Betsy said. "At considerable risk to ourselves, I might add."

She spoke slowly and with emphasis as she clutched her cloth grocery bag in both hands, an eyebrow arched above an unyielding gaze.

"There's been a whole lot of nonsense, honestly, and I've had about enough explosions for one day," she said.

"The governors didn't want to let us leave," Theodore said. "I thought we were goners."

"In any case, you've made a good many promises, Eb," Grandma Betsy said.

At this, the D1 unit stepped forward, its blue eyes shining.

"I believe," it said. "It is within your power to update my programming and allow me to set my own goals, rather than be a servant to the whims of others."

As the robot finished speaking, Gary stretched and stood to his full height, his furry head brushing the ceiling.

"I," he said. "Bring news of your impacts on the Northlands. Because many are drawn to Centrum City, few people maintain the countryside, and much of the infrastructure has been overrun by forests. Without repairs, old lanterns and generators are slowly damaging the wildlife, and I fear the region may eventually become uninhabitable."

"I see," Eb said.

The Luminary adjusted his glasses, then tapped the air with gloved fingers. He made a twisting motion with his hand, then paused, nodding to Gary.

"Go on," he said.

"For many years," the bigfoot said. "I've been salvaging everything I can from the homes and ghost towns that have been left to the elements. I've even recovered a B3 unit that was torn apart by animals."

The mannequin reached up and rubbed Gary's furry shoulder.

"He would greatly appreciate a bit of assistance," it said. "If I'm not speaking out of turn."

"And perhaps," Gary said. "If I draw people to the region with my collected curiosities, they might recognize the beauty of the snowy evergreens and see there's something worth saving."

Projections played across the lenses of the Luminary's glasses, and he briefly took them off, rubbing his nose.

"For my part, I'd simply appreciate access to the library and its vast collection of knowledge," the mannequin said.

Eb sighed and poured himself tea from a gooseneck kettle.

"I can appreciate your varied challenges, such as they are," he said. "I've found no shortage of problems in Um."

"These people have done a great deal to advance your agenda, Eb," Oja said.

She turned the seat of a padded swivel chair in a circle with her finger.

"You should know," she said. "The Governors believe humans were involved in Governor Eyebright's death."

"It was an accident," Theodore said.

"They hit him with their vehicle upon their entry into Um," Eb said. "It was a confluence of energetic events drawn together. A cosmic nexus. An improbable convergence."

"The Governors are unlikely to believe that," Oja said.

She walked to the drinks cart and swirled the gooseneck kettle, pouring herself Earl Grey in a cup that matched the Luminary's.

"The Governors won't take issue with things they don't know about," Eb said.

"A bold statement," Oja said.

She swirled her cup, then held it to her lips, blowing across surface tension.

"I've been told," Eb said. "That more pressing matters await. A little birdie told me I had offers of marriage."

"Purely for the purposes of providing you with the rights afforded to any member of elven society," Oja said.

"Two souls eternally intertwined for strictly business reasons?" Eb asked.

"Precisely."

Grandma Betsy coughed, and the Luminary turned to her, picking up his glasses.

"Yes?" he asked.

"Your city is under attack," Grandma Betsy said.

"And you said your spaceship would take us back to Wisconsin," Theodore said.

Light shining from the lenses, Eb slipped on his custom spectacles and waved to his Z7 unit.

"Yes, yes," he said. "Everything you've said is true, Betsy Judith Lyman. And as it is certainly within my power to grant the requests of your tagalongs, you can consider everything approved."

The Luminary snapped his fingers, and the robot in the leather coat walked to the door, motioning for the mannequin and the D1 unit and Gary to follow, which they did, waving as they went.

"I do appreciate your freeing me from my life in an abandoned clothing store," the mannequin said.

"And I appreciate the gift of free will immensely," the D1 unit said.

"If you come this way again," Gary said. "I hope you'll pay a visit to the Northlands."

Theodore held up his hand and watched them go, feeling the regret of a last day of school or the end of a slumber party.

"Oja?" Eb asked.

"Eb?" she asked.

"I've promised these good people a ride home by way of a saucer designed to ride the dimensional aether."

"So I've gathered," Oja said.

She sipped her tea, then set the cup on a cork board coaster on the conference room table.

"To that end, would you do me a favor?" Eb asked.

"Depends on the favor," Oja said.

"Could you make sure none of your determined countrymen find their way into the building within the next few minutes?"

Oja nodded, braids swaying as she strolled from the room, a hand to her sword hilt.

"I'll hold down the fort," she said.

The door closed, and Eb pressed several buttons on a wall keypad.

"While I trust my security measures, it never hurts to take a few extra precautions," he said.

"I always check the stove twice," Grandma Betsy said. "Every time I leave the house."

"Yes," Eb said. "Without question. Incidentally, you do still have the boots?"

"Of course," Grandma Betsy said. "In my cloth bag, underneath my hat and gloves."

"Good, good," Eb said. "Make sure you have them both, because in its current configuration, the ship won't work without them."

"Done," Grandma Betsy said. "And done."

"And don't forget to press the red button when you get home," Eb said.

"The boots have a red button?"
"On the cube," Eb said.
"The cube," Grandma Betsy said. "Yes, the cube."
"That's the most important part," Eb said.
The wall at the back of the room slid open, and Eb again led the way through long hallways and workshops and labs to the hangar where the levitating saucer waited, this time without cable harnesses holding it in place. It hung in the air in much the same way as a ladder stands on its own, waiting for use, and with wires and external tubing concealed by gleaming panels, Eb paused only to open a service hatch. He connected alligator clips to the dead governor's boots, cinched everything down, then shut the compartment before opening the crew hatch and wishing Theodore and Grandma Betsy a pleasant goodbye.

The Lake Incident

Beneath Theodore's feet, the floor of the saucer rocked, gently, like a boat. Near the front of the craft, on the side that had the main field projector, a console monitor lit up with camera views of the front and sides and back of the vehicle. Electrical cables and pressurized hoses connected to blocky modules that looked like mushrooms attached to trees. A second monitor lit up; text scrolled like a computer booting. The seats themselves were comfortable enough, better than the one time Theodore had flown on an airplane. These seats had five-point harnesses and thick, leather cushions.

"Where's the steering wheel?" Theodore asked.

"I don't think we're the ones driving," Grandma Betsy said.

Theodore held the backpack with Calipso in it, and a speaker crackled overhead. On the second monitor, Eb appeared seated at a desk in a small office.

"The capacitor bank for the initial burst is charging," he said. "Magnetic holds decoupling. Easing craft into dimensional substrate in 10 seconds."

In front of the saucer, the air shimmered, and the hangar wall turned to fog.

"I wonder how many times I lost something," Grandma Betsy said. "And it found its way to Um."

"It's a dimension between dimensions," Eb said. "As I've said, it exists everywhere nobody's looking, in every daydream and every tree that falls with no one to hear it."

The saucer slid into the fog and accelerated, speeding through the same billowing whiteness that had taken Grandma Betsy's Chevy Celebrity from the snowy Wisconsin highway to the hilly Boffin Northlands. The video monitor cut to black, and the speaker turned to static.

"It's hard to tell how fast we're going," Theodore said.

"It's like an airplane flying through cloud cover," Grandma Betsy said.

"Or running around in fogged-up goggles."

The saucer vibrated as it flew, and through his coat sleeves, Theodore felt Calipso pawing at the insides of the backpack. An overhead fan blew warm air from heater coils; Grandma Betsy unzipped her coat.

"By my count," she said. "Tomorrow is New Year's Eve. Your parents will be flying back."

"Calipso doesn't like it in the bag," Theodore said.

"I wouldn't either," Grandma Betsy said. "But it shouldn't be too much longer."

Theodore imagined the saucer as a skipped rock skimming the surface of a lake, a stone springing across surface tension, and as he felt his eyes growing heavy, sleepiness rolling in on the cozy mists that hung between worlds, the saucer shuddered, twice, and a hissing sound filled the cabin.

"Grandma?" he asked.

"Either we're going very fast," Grandma Betsy said. "Or what we hit was going very fast. You can see where it went straight through the ship."

She pointed, and light streamed through matching holes the size of golf balls in the steel flooring.

"That's not good," Theodore said.

As he spoke, another volley punched through the front window, narrowly avoiding the seats as sparks shot from a sheared cable.

"Maybe this is why Eb let us go first," Theodore said.

After a few seconds of bright flashes and blinking consoles, the lights inside the saucer went out entirely.

"He did refer to us," Grandma Betsy said. "As test pilots."

Outside, the fog flickered, becoming darker as tiny white feathers broke away, swirling across the front window.

"I think," Grandma Betsy said. "I think we've come out of it."

It took Theodore a few seconds to realize that the feathers were snow that was coming down as thick, swirling flakes, and he would later learn that they'd returned to the same variety of Wisconsin blizzard they'd departed from, the second one in less than a week.

"I still wonder how fast we're going," Theodore said.

"Entirely too fast, I'd imagine," Grandma Betsy said.

Had they smashed immediately into a brick wall or the stony bluffs that overlooked the Mississippi, the results would likely have been tragic, but grandmothers and grandsons returning home from strange adventures rarely have that kind of luck. As one bit of foresight, Eb had built shock absorbers into the seats, and he'd designed the frame of the saucer to direct the impact of a crash away from its occupants. Coupled with the fact that Theodore and his grandmother didn't know they were plummeting towards the frozen surface of Lake Onalaska, the ship punched a hole in the ice without inflicting more than bruises, and only then from the seat harnesses, on its passengers.

"There's water coming in through the holes," Theodore said.

"I'll get Calipso," Grandma Betsy said.

"It's hard to see," Theodore said.

"Pull the hatch release," Grandma Betsy said. "To the left of the window."

By the time they scrambled out onto the deep snow of the lake, the saucer was mostly submerged and sinking fast. Dense accumulation and blowing winds made for low visibility, and due to the white-out, it felt unlikely that anyone had witnessed the crash.

"I think I can see the shore," Theodore said.

A red light blinked in the distance, and they trudged towards it, a merry glow that eventually became the sign for a raft rental business that was closed for the season.

"Why, I know where we are," Grandma Betsy said. "Your grandfather took your cousins out in a pontoon three summers ago."

Snow continued blowing and swirling, but now that Grandma Betsy had her sense of direction, she led Theodore to the road and, despite the heavy flakes, walked along the northern shoreline to a bar and grill that was, miraculously, despite the late hour and the inclement weather, open.

"I think it's best," Grandma Betsy said. "If we don't say too much about what's happened the last few days."

Theodore gave a thumbs up and stomped snow from his boots on the entryway mats.

"People might get the wrong idea about what we're saying," he said.

"They'd think we're crazy," Grandma Betsy said.

The restaurant side of Evergreen Beer and Burgers was empty, but a middle-aged woman with a Brenda name tag pushed through swinging doors and pulled menus from a host podium.

"Table for two?" she asked.

"Yes, please," Grandma Betsy said. "A cup of coffee for me. And I'll probably have a piece of pie. Do you have pie?"

"We have cherry and pecan."

"I'll take cherry, then," Grandma Betsy said. "Would you like anything, Theodore?"

Brenda guided her customers to a booth, and Theodore shook the snow from his jacket as he slipped off the backpack.

"I'll have a hot chocolate," he said.

"If it's not too much trouble," Grandma Betsy said. "We're a bit stranded, and my cell phone is dead. May I use your phone?"

It was in this way that Grandma Betsy got ahold of Hazel Torgeson, whom she'd met many years earlier at a book club, and Hazel showed up to the Evergreen 30 minutes later in an aging Prius to drive them back to Grandma Betsy's house on the bluffs.

"You're lucky," Hazel said. "Another hour or so and I would've been in bed."

At home, Calipso, excited to be released from her long imprisonment in the backpack, disappeared immediately down the carpeted basement stairs, and Grandma Betsy discovered that the other cats had pushed a bag of food off the counter and made a mess of things on the kitchen floor. Other than that, the house was the same as it had always been. The grandfather clock ticked in the living room. A thermometer hung against the outer glass of the bay window. The furnace kicked on, and pipes groaned when the sink faucet ran too long.

"You'll need to be in bed, soon," Grandma Betsy said.

"I know," Theodore said.

Now that the headlights of Hazel's Prius had disappeared down the driveway, Theodore took pens and paper from the desk in the study, determined to write down a list of his adventures, while Grandma Betsy, having poured hot water onto decaf grounds in the french press, sat down for her second cup of the day.

"Make sure your boots don't drip on the rug," she said.

"They're on the bathroom heater," Theodore said.

Coffee cooling, Grandma Betsy reached into her coat pocket and withdrew the cube Eb had given her in the library conference room. The top had a glass circle, and the sides included beveled rings around golden keys and switches, but only one face had a big, red button. She sipped her drink, then paused for a moment, her finger hovering impulsively in the air, before she pressed down.

The cube wiggled, then levitated above the place mats, light pulsing from the top. Then, noiselessly, as Grandma Betsy drummed her fingers on the table, the cube began to spin.

Acknowledgments

Thank you to the many people who listened to me read early versions of the first few chapters of this book. Thank you to the third grade classes at Robbins Elementary and Sherman Elementary who loved the Wonderful Wizard of Oz and inspired me (without knowing it) to keep writing. Thank you to Lou and Ann for encouraging me. Thank you to my folks, Carolyn and Joe, Chris and Ruth, for being family. Thank you to Ginger McCall for inspiring me to be a better human being. And, of course, thank you to Pura for reading.

Many people have been helpful along the way. Thanks to Bob and Jyl for letting me bounce ideas around. Thank you to Stash for being a sounding board. I appreciate people like Rob Reed, who I met in the '80s at the Eau Claire Public Library (and who was kind enough to look over this manuscript and give some feedback). Thank you to Nora, Arne, Mindy, Jake, Uncle Todd, Alissa, Brendan and Anne, Ken, Jon, Abe, Ian, Skip, Paul and Veronica, Greg Power, Jake Donze, and the many other people who have listened to me talk about some aspect of this project.

Finally, I want to acknowledge the inspiration I drew from L. Frank Baum's The Wonderful Wizard of Oz and its plot structure. While most books take characters on a journey, Dorothy's adventures have a fantastic symmetry that keeps readers smiling and turning pages in a way more authors should try to emulate. The success of Baum's writing is due in no small part to parents enjoying reading books to their children at bedtime; to readers who have enjoyed reading The Sublime Luminary of Um, I encourage them to go back to the Oz books, for if a cyclone had not plucked a house from the Kansas prairie, my own work would certainly not exist.